SCHIRMER'S HEADHUNTERS

Also by Leo Kessler

In the SS Assault Regiment Wotan series

Leo Kessler

Schirmer's
Headhunters

Macdonald Futura Publishers

A Futura Book

First published in Great Britain in 1981
by Macdonald Futura Publishers Ltd

ISBN 0 7088 2063 8
Photoset by
Rowland Phototypesetting Ltd
Bury St Edmunds, Suffolk
Printed and bound in Great Britain by
©ollins, Glasgow

Macdonald Futura Publishers Ltd
Paulton House, 8 Shepherdess Walk
London N1 7LW

Author's Note

The headhunters, that is what they had called themselves. *Die Kopfjaeger* – the headhunters – and that is exactly what they had been in the steaming, tropical jungle. Lying, racked with pain in his chipped hospital cot in a shabby Bavarian infirmary run by the brothers of the local workhouse, ex-Colonel Schirmer had insisted that if ever I wrote anything about his experiences in Indo-China in the '50's, I should call his men just that.

'Because that is what they were – shitting headhunters for the piss-assed Frogs,' he had croaked, already a little drunk on the bottle of whisky he had ordered me to smuggle in behind the backs of the pious, brown-habited brothers – 'A lot of warm brothers who spend all their time playing five against one in their cells,' he had sneered at them. – 'Paid by those white-gloved pansies in Saigon to sabre off the yellow heads of those treacherous slant-eyed shits! . . . *Headhunters, out for blood!*' He had roared with laughter in that outrageous manner of his, but his roar had ended in a choking fit that had racked his yellow, emaciated frame, and he had begun to vomit blood.

'And by the Great God and all his shitting triangles, didn't we just saw off their slant-eyed turnips,' he had continued the following day, his angry, bitter energy still undampened by the powerful drugs which the permanently shocked brothers had been pumping into his wasted body all night. 'Out there, we waded through their blood right up to our thighs. Hell, we raped their virgins for breakfast and bayoneted their little brothers for supper!'

He had seen the look on my face and sniggered, 'Now don't look like that, Kessler, as if you've just discovered that you've shat yerself! What do you think it was like out there in Indo-China, eh – a pissing convent-girl outing,

with us keeping our knees tight together in case someone
wants to put his dirty big paw up our skirts to have a feel?
Ner,' he had taken a deep slug of this day's bottle of
whisky, half-draining it, 'out there it was the kind of war
that a pen-pusher like you, Kessler, couldn't *even* begin to
imagine in a month of shitting Sundays! It was kill or be
killed!'

'You know, Kessler,' he had continued, his voice more
reasonable and reflective, 'I have had the great privilege
of seeing three empires die.' He had smiled at me sardoni-
cally. 'Hitler's, in Russia – by God, didn't those Ivan
sub-humans give us supermen a nasty kick up the ass
there! I saw the Tommies lose theirs at Suez in '56 – oh
yes, Kessler, I was there too, you know. A 300-year old
empire lost between cups of stinking tea.' He had
laughed, but there had been no humour in his faded blue
eyes. 'The niggers deserved to have taken it off them. But
that was nothing compared to what happened in Indo-
China when the Frogs lost theirs. My God, Kessler, that
was something when we were the Headhunters fighting
those treacherous yellow Slant-eyes up and down the
peninsula. That was the dirty war to end all dirty wars!'
His eyes had suddenly flashed with fire, but the rest of the
whisky had soon doused that fire and soon he'd relapsed
into incoherent, mad muttering and mumbling.

This, then, is the story of Colonel Schirmer's
mercenaries; the countless bitter renegades who fought
France's dirty war for her and died in the jungles of
Indo-China – *the story of Schirmer's Headhunters* . . .

One: Massacre Valley

ONE

Colonel Schirmer thrust his camouflaged kepi to the back of his big, scarred, shaven head and stared down at the terrain below. In the fading light there wasn't much to see.

Two bare ridge-lines, almost parallel, were sticking up barren and brown through the usual lush-green canopy of Indo-Chinese tropical jungle. Running north to south, a little closer together at the northern end, they marked the boundaries of the twenty-kilometre-long valley in which his Headhunters – of the Foreign Legion's Special Para Battalion – would soon commence their march into the unknown.

Involuntarily, the big ex-SS colonel with the bold scar-red face, tanned a deep leathery-brown by the tropical sun, shivered despite the wet heat. In the last eight years since he and his bunch of renegade SS paras had been forced into fighting France's dirty war* in Indo-China for her, he had flown over thousands of similar canopies but he had never been able to throw off the ominous feeling of dread whenever they approached a new one.

There were always the same old questions to which there were no answers, save those written in hot blood. What did the jungle hide? How many unfriendly brown Slant-eyes were watching the fleet of choppers pass at this very moment? Who or what was responsible for those faint wisps of grey smoke at the far end of the long, narrow valley? And what was waiting for them down there in what the awed, frightened, Frog stubble-hoppers

*See *Hellfire* for further details.

were now beginning to call 'Massacre Valley'?

'*Massacre Valley*,' Schirmer licked his suddenly dry lips and mouthed the name silently to himself as the fleet of choppers began to come down, their radios already crackling noisily. The name was appropriate enough. Twice in the last month, battalion-strength strike forces of the French Army had crossed the Red River and had marched north into the valley below, heading for the war-torn country's frontier with China. Their objective had been to find out what the Chinese-supported Viet Minh rebels were up to. Uncle Ho* had not staged a single major action against the Frogs since Christmas, 1953. Now it was February, 1954, and the monsoon season was only three months away, when all ops would have to cease. And twice the Frog stubble-hoppers had disappeared somewhere down there without trace.

'*Merde, alors*!' one-armed Colonel Mercier, the Legion's political adviser and France's secret strong-man in Indo-China, had cursed at his last briefing for the mission. 'Nearly two thousand men cannot disappear without trace, Schirmer! *Impossible*!'

The plump, red-faced, cunning-eyed Frenchman had glared at the big, bronzed German whose camouflaged blouse bore no decoration or badge of rank save the cloth wings of a Legion para and the tarnished silver runes of the SS and spluttered, 'The legs' – he used the Legion's contemptuous term for the Infantry – 'are shitting their drawers in fear. Massacre Valley they call the place.' He blew out his lips under the trim military moustache in Gallic disgust. 'They'd rather shoot their officers in the back than go up there. But no matter, Schirmer, they won't have to. Instead you'll take *your* bunch of Boche cut-throats into the valley and find out what's going on. What I – and the High Command pansies – want to know is what is so important about that damned bit of jungle that makes Uncle Ho want to take on two battalions of regular French troops while the whole of the delta, full of tempting targets, is left in peace. There is something going on up there in the north, Schirmer, mark my words – something shittingly well unpleasant.'

*Ho Chi Minh, chief of the Viet Minh rebellion.

'Schirmer!'

The German colonel took his eyes off the jungle looming up ever larger and turned round.

It was White Lightning, his American second-in-command. Nature had played an evil trick on Washington Lee Lincoln Lightning, formerly of the US 101st Airborne Division before he had killed a superior officer and been forced to desert. His face, despite the lidless eyes, was straight from an Army recruiting poster – keen and hard, with a finely chiselled nose and a lean, tough jaw – perfect, save for one thing: from birth he had not had one single hair on his body. Lacking eyebrows, facial or body hair, he was completely and utterly bald – hence his nickname.

'What is it, Major?' Schirmer snapped, forgetting Massacre Valley and Colonel Mercier abruptly.

'Point ship just radioed no sign of enemy activity,' the American answered in his cool efficient manner. 'If there are any gooks down there, they're pretty well hidden.'

'They always are, Major. Take the usual precautions. We go in at an angle to the smoke flare. No landing. All troopers to drop out at five metres, and warn everyone to look out for those damned punji sticks.'*

'Wilco, Skipper,' the American answered and hurried up the swaying helicopter to where the command radio operator was waiting.

Sergeant-Major Schulze, the Headhunters' senior NCO, thrust his pornographic magazine into his pack with a sigh. 'Why all the fuss, Colonel?' he said with a lazy grin on his broad, good-humoured, Hamburg face. 'One good blast from my fart cannon, after all that pea-soup we had yesterday, and I'd blast Uncle Ho and all his Slant-eyes from here to Moscow.'

Schirmer smiled and started buckling on his helmet. 'Yes, you big rogue, that's what I've been thinking all the way here. I'm surprised the damn chopper's still flying.' His voice hardened. 'All right, Headhunters, prepare to land!'

Now all was swift, purposeful activity in the command

---

*Bamboo stakes, sharpened and dipped in human faeces, used to inflict infected wounds in the foot of anyone stepping on them.

helicopter. The hardened veterans of six years of fighting in Europe and eight years in Asia slapped machine-pistol magazines to check they were securely fixed, heaved their packs higher on their shoulders, grabbed hold of the hand-holds, held their breath and prepared to bale out.

Schirmer poised at the door, the wind whipping his uniform tight against his lean, muscular body. Suddenly his blouse was damp with sweat from the heat coming up from the green mass of the jungle. He looked down, his stomach tightening as it always did at this moment. Were they going to land right in the middle of the Slant-eyes? He swallowed hard and dismissed the dread thought.

The command pilot eased back on the cyclic. The helicopter's nose came up. Speed dropped until they were almost hovering. The chopper started to vibrate crazily, as if it would fall apart at any moment. Long grass, flattened by the prop blast, and the grey stream of the smoke marker appeared suddenly.

'*DZ*!' Schirmer yelled above the racket.

The Headhunters rose as one and shuffled towards the open door. Schirmer tried to dismiss the thought that at this very moment one of the Slant-eyes might be drawing a bead on him as he crouched there. He raised his right thumb, to signify that they were right above the dropping zone.

They were about twenty metres above the ground. He threw a glance upwards. The blue spurts of exhaust flames were everywhere; the racket was impossible. The whole battalion was dead on target. Fifteen metres . . . Ten metres . . . He could wait no longer. The chopper was virtually at stalling speed. He drew a deep breath. '*ALLES FUER DEUTSCHLAND*!'* He gave the old *Waffen SS* war-cry and flung himself out of the door.

Colonel Schirmer hit the ground hard, rolled over and came up, grease-gun at the ready. All around him in the swirling, elephant grass and whirling leaves, thrown up in a mad dance by the roaring choppers' rotors, the Headhunters were slamming to the deck, completing the same roll and dashing for the cover of the tree-line, weapons at the alert.

*Everything for Germany.

'*First Company, ready to march*!' a coarse, beery voice sang out to his right. That would be Spider-Arse, officially Lieutenant Kurtz, a survivor of the old 666th SS Para Battalion.

'*Second Company, ready to march*!' Lieutenant Thiel, formerly of the *Bodyguard*, cried somewhere to Schirmer's front.

Schirmer nodded his approval, but still he didn't relax his hold on the grease-gun and his eyes searched the jungle for the slightest sign of suspicious movement.

'The girls of the Third, ready to sway their delicate, sweet little bottoms!' an affected, feminine voice shrilled. Schirmer grinned despite his inner tension. Lieutenant 'Pansy' Petersen, formerly of the *Death's Head*, holder of the Knight's Cross and Oak Leaves, was running true to form.

'Colonel Schirmer, sir,' Tod's sickly whine cut through the racket close to the CO's ear.

Schirmer spun round to face Tod, the ex-Gestapo man, who was officially the Headhunter's political officer but whose real function was still that of torturer. Involuntarily Schirmer wrinkled his nose in disgust. The sallow-faced, bespectacled officer with the wet, slack, drooling lips was crouched there, as if he expected to be shot by a Slant-eye at any moment, his splay-fingered hands playing nervously with his good-luck charm: a tobacco-pouch made from the tanned skin of a negress's breast, complete with dun-coloured nipple.

'What is it, Tod?' he snapped irritably.

'I've just found something, sir.'

'I'll piss in my boot,' Schirmer roared above the racket as the choppers, having dropped their cargoes, were beginning to rise once more. 'What – one of those juicy-arsed little boys' bums you drool over?'

'No, no, not that, sir,' the ex-schoolmaster answered hastily, blushing a deep-red with embarrassment. 'You know I'm almost normal. I would never – '

'Piss or get off the pot, man,' Schirmer interrupted him brutally. 'What have you found?'

'Footprints, sir.'

'What!'

Tod repeated what he had just said and, tugging

Schirmer's sleeve, led him to a spot a couple of metres away. 'There,' he announced, pointing at the trampled grass. 'And they can't be from our Legion boots. Those are the marks of their sandals!'

Colonel Erwin Schirmer did not need to be told who 'they' were, for already he could smell the stench of *nuóu-mán*, that nauseating, rotten fish-paste the Slant-eyes used to season their rice; there was no mistaking it.

'Slant-eyes, Skipper?' White Lightning's calm voice asked quietly behind him.

Schirmer nodded grimly, as the sound of the departing choppers began to die away and vanish altogether. 'Looks like it, Major,' he said slowly.

'What now, sir?' Tod quavered, eyeing the jungle ahead through his gold-rimmed spectacles with undisguised apprehension.

For what seemed a long time, Schirmer did not answer. The other two waited, no sound disturbing the silence now save the rustle of the damp tropical breeze in the trees. Finally Schirmer shook his head like a man coming out of a deep sleep and said quietly, 'What now you ask, Tod? What else can we mercenaries do but march, fight and die.' He raised his voice harshly, 'All right, you dogs of death, do you want to live forever?' he bellowed. '*Headhunters – advance!*'

Five minutes later the jungle and the night had swallowed them up completely. *The march into Massacre Valley had commenced . .*

TWO

'Puffs, pansies and pederasts!' Colonel Mercier cursed to himself, wrinkling his nose up at the overpowering odour of perfume which filled the high, elegant, white-and-gold antechamber. He ran his one hand over his grizzled cropped head and stared in disgust at the immaculately uniformed staff officers who filled the place, telling himself the whole damned headquarters was full of idle perverts.

Sitting stiff-backed and isolated from the rest, the Legion colonel thought once again that if the war in Indo-China were lost, it would not be due to a lack of fighting spirit at the front but because of the attitudes of these foppish, uniformed fools in Saigon and their pink political bosses back in Paris. How often had he come to this same HQ over the last bloody years to hear the latest 'master' plan expounded, immaculate to the last detail, just as the planners were immaculate. Le Clerc, De Lattre, Salan – they all had had great plans, full of promise, but all based on European conditions, with the Continent's road systems and communications, not on the virtually impassable jungles of northern Indo-China. Inevitably, the great plans had ended in failure and the planners had been forced to go. Now it was Navarre's turn. He, too, thought he could beat Uncle Ho and General Giap* with his fortified 'hedgehogs' up in the north. Indeed, it was common gossip in the senior officers' mess that Navarre believed he had already beaten the rebels; had there not been any incidents, save the disappearance of the two strike-battalions, since January? But to Colonel Mercier, the very absence of rebel activity proved that something was going on. Indo-China was *too* quiet.

*Commander-in-Chief of the rebels.

'Colonel, the General will see you now,' an affected St Cyr voice broke into his reveries.

Mercier glared at the foppish young aide, his skinny shoulders seemingly bowed under the gold-braided aide-de-camp's lanyard. 'Thank you,' he barked and, picking up his kepi and white gloves, which were de rigueur at HQ, followed the man's mincing steps.

Navarre stopped stroking the siamese cat which purred on the top of his massive Louis Quinze desk and smiled at the colonel, though his dark eyes above the hook of a nose did not light up. '*Ah, mon cher Mercier de la Légion,*' he exclaimed. 'But please take a seat, old fellow.' He indicated one of the stiff-backed antique chairs with a wave of a well-manicured hand.

The fellow has the fragrance of the eighteenth century about him, Mercier told himself, as Navarre reached over for a cigarette to place in his long, ivory cigarette holder.

'Now then, Mercier,' the general said with fake bonhommie after he had lit the gold-tipped, hand-rolled cigarette, 'where's the fire, eh?'

'Here,' Mercier said bluntly, sitting bolt-upright in the stiff-backed chair.

Navarre seemed amused. 'Why, Indo-China has never been quieter,' he said.

'Exactly.'

'What is that supposed to mean, my dear chap?' Navarre asked.

Mercier looked at him. He had seen Navarre's predecessors behind that self-same desk with that self-same look of absolute confidence on their smug faces, fully believing they had won the war while Uncle Ho was planning yet another stroke to bring down French power in the Far East.

'I have been here since 1945, General, and without flattering myself,' Mercier answered. 'I think I can almost feel when the Viets are up to something.' He tapped the side of his long nose with his one hand. 'I trust this and not what air reconnaissance reports.'

Navarre laughed easily. 'Well, I'm afraid this time, my dear fellow, your nose, admirable as I am sure it is, has absorbed the wrong odour.'

He rose to his feet, cuddling the siamese cat under his

left arm, and pointed at the large map of Indo-China behind his desk, which was covered with a rash of blue and red marks. 'Look at it, Mercier. My fortified hedgehogs cover the whole of the north, interdicting all the roads leading to China, and at the same time they serve as bases for disruptive raids on enemy centres and supply routes. Let Uncle Ho attack them if he wishes. Why, the hedgehog at Dien Bien Phu alone would eat up a whole division of Viet troops, if not more.' He beamed at a stony-faced Colonel Mercier. 'Give me one more year here, my dear chap, and I shall be ready to go over to the offensive. In 1955 I shall finish with Uncle Ho once and for all.'

'*1955, mon Général*!' Mercier exploded. 'Do you think Uncle Ho will wait that long, especially now that Giap is receiving all that American equipment captured from them by the Chinese in Korea!'

Navarre was unmoved by Mercier's outburst. Calmly he stroked the purring cat and sat down again. 'So,' he said, 'and what can Uncle Ho do with that equipment, especially as we interdict all the roads from the north. Tell me that, my dear Mercier?'

'I can't, General, that's the damned annoying part of it. But this calm and the disappearance of the two strike battalions worry me. There is something going on,' Mercier said a little desperately. 'I *know* it!'

Navarre smiled at the little Legion colonel indulgently. 'A little bird tells me that you have sent those Boche killers of yours into the north, Mercier,' he said.

'Someone should strangle that particular canary,' Mercier snarled. 'There is far too much loose talk at this headquarters, General.'

'It is the nature of the staff, Mercier. Staff officers are given to gossip like elderly maiden ladies in a provincial village. But, tell me, what do you hope to achieve with these Boche fellows, eh?'

Suddenly the languid tone had vanished from Navarre's voice and Mercier knew why. The commanding general did not approve of the Headhunters' special methods. Obviously they were too much for his delicate stomach.

'They have two objectives, sir,' Mercier replied, iron in his voice, ready as always to defend the battalion which he had raised eight years before and which he regarded as a kind of personal armed force to be used for his own long-range plans. 'One, to discover what happened to those two missing battalions. Two –' He hesitated.

'Go on, Mercier, spit it out.'

'Two, sir, to attempt to find out what the enemy's intentions are.'

The languid tone vanished from Navarre's voice. 'Mercier, I have already told you that we have virtually beaten the enemy. My strategy is working. You are behaving like an old woman seeing burglars under every bed.'

Mercier flushed but said nothing.

'All right. You have sent your Boches out and it is too late to stop the move.' He looked directly at a red-faced Mercier. 'But I tell you this. If they run into trouble up there in the north, they'll have to get themselves out of it or take the consequences. I'm not wasting any good French lives to rescue a bunch of Boche cut-throats. Is that understood, Mercier?'

Mercier fought to control himself. '*Entendu, mon Général,*' he replied, the words almost strangling him.

'*Bon!*' Navarre stopped fondling the cat and looked down at his papers. 'You may go now, Colonel.'

Mercier clicked to attention, telling himself that he had made a mess of things. Now Schirmer, two hundred kilometres from the nearest French base, and deep in the heart of the rebel-held territory, was on his own. Navarre would not even let him have choppers to pull him and his Headhunters out. If Schirmer ran into trouble now, he'd have to fight his way out on foot in some of the toughest terrain in the world.

'*Shit, shit, shit,*' he cursed furiously to himself, but to Navarre he said, '*Bonjour, mon Général!*' and strode to the door.

General Navarre did not even look up, but the siamese cat purred happily and looked at him with a look of smug triumph on its stupid feline face.

THREE

'Four o'clock, sir,' Schulze whispered and placed his heavy hand on Schirmer's shoulder cautiously. He knew the CO. He always slept with his .45 under his head; and in the last eight years in Indo-China, Schirmer, like the rest of the Headhunters, had learned to shoot first and ask questions afterwards.

'Thanks, Schulze,' the CO answered, awake at once.

For a moment he lay there, listening to the pre-dawn noises of the jungle – a frond calling, a nut bouncing down, the night animals silent now while the day birds had not yet begun to call – running his mind over the previous day and the tasks of the new one.

They had been in Massacre Valley for twenty-four hours now, yet apart from those mysterious footprints, they had seen no sign of human activity. All the same, Schirmer's sixth sense told him they were being watched. Twice he had caught a whiff of *nuoa-man*, a sure indicator that there were Slant-eyes around somewhere; and during the midday heat when the jungle tiger slept, they had heard a tiger call.

'Yeah, jungle cat, he have two legs,' White Lightning had commented grimly, an observation to which Schirmer could only nod his head in agreement.

They were being watched all right, but why? Schirmer dismissed the problem. He sat up, shivering a little in the pre-dawn cold. Reaching into his pack, he took out some of the pre-cooked rice which was the Headhunters' basic ration, sprinkled it with dried pineapple chunks and sugar and ate two quick handfuls of the dry mixture before adding water from his canteen to the *vinogel* wine-paste and taking a deep drink. The fiery red *pinard* exploded in his stomach like a bomb and he could feel the new energy surge through his stiff limbs at once. Colonel Schirmer's day could start.

'Schulze,' he commanded, rising to his feet, 'get the water parties out.'

'Sir.'

'Every man to take two salt tablets. It's going to be a hot day.'

'Heaven, arse and cloudburst, what wouldn't I give for half o'litre of good Bavarian suds,' Schulze moaned, swigging down the rest of his pinard, 'instead of this frog cat's piss!'

'Get on with it,' Schirmer said with a grin and started to walk over to where White Lightning was buckling on his equipment, while the first water party of ten men made their way through the bushes to the nearby stream to carry out their body functions and fill their canteens for the long march ahead that day. But Colonel Schirmer did not reach the American.

Abruptly the thick pre-dawn silence was broken by a shrill scream of agony. Schirmer spun round. One of the first water party staggered to the nearest tree, grabbing it for support with frantic fingers, a great arrow protruding from his belly from which spilled blood and undigested rice in horrid confusion.

'*Take cover*!' Schirmer yelled, as the man pitched to the ground and the second arrow hissed through the gloom to strike another Headhunter in the shoulder.

As one the Headhunters flung themselves to the earth, packs in front of them, weapons ready and cocked. In that same instant there was a pop like a champagne cork. Schirmer threw a look upwards. A star shell exploded right above the Headhunters' position and bathed the glade in a brilliant, phosphorescent, eerie glow.

'*Slant-eyes*!' Schirmer yelled, knowing now from the shell that the arrows had not come from some marauding jungle natives but from Uncle Ho's boys.

Behind him, White Lightning called, 'Three Company – *à moi*!'

'Come on, girls,' Pansy Petersen rallied his shaken men. 'Remember your lieutenant has got a hole in his arse!'

Schirmer nodded his approval. White Lightning was carrying out standard operating procedure. While the two lead companies let themselves be held down by the ambush, he was withdrawing with the other one to attempt to take the unseen enemy by the rear. He raised his head cautiously, peering along the line of trees and seeing nothing.

'Companies One and Two,' he commanded, 'give Slant-eyes a burst, but don't waste yer lead!'

The men needed no urging. Four hundred weapons crashed into action. Wood splintered, palm fronds came down in a green rain, richochets howled and the air was filled with a sound like the humming of a million angry hornets. Schirmer let his men fire a full ten seconds – it gave them an opportunity to get rid of their fear and rage – before yelling, 'All right, all right, cease fire – *NOW*!'

Again he stared along the line of scarred and shattered trees in the last light of the falling star shell, automatically noting that White Lightning's force had already disappeared into the jungle to his rear. He could see nothing. Whoever had ambushed them was not showing himself. Slowly and reluctantly he rose to his feet and stood there, fully exposed, feeling his flesh crawl at the thought of that long pronged arrow that might penetrate his body at any moment. Nothing happened. Their ambushers seemingly did not want the tempting target. Had they already vanished deep into the jungle? If so, what had been the purpose of the attack? Why reveal their presence just to wing a couple of men? He shook his head in puzzled annoyance and called, 'Schulze, *à moi – at the double now*!' He thrust his forty-five into his belt for a quick draw and jammed his grease-gun under his right arm. 'All right, you big rogue, let's go and have a look-see.'

'Why do they allus pick on the little shits?' Schulze asked in mock dismay, but he followed his beloved CO willingly enough, as he left the line of prostrate, tense Headhunters and broke into the shattered trees.

Grease-guns at the ready, the two Headhunters prowled cautiously through the green gloom of the forest, still heavy with the stink of cordite, Schulze covering Schirmer's back. It took them five minutes to discover the depression in the elephant grass where the archer had lain who had attacked them. But there was only one.

Schirmer cursed and said, 'I don't know, Schulze, what in three devils' name is going on? What kind of crazy business is this when one lone Slant-eyes attacks a whole battalion of the Legion?'

'Don't ask me, sir,' was all that Schulze could reply. 'I've given up trying to puzzle out the Slant-eyes years ago. I can't even make sense of their slits – and that's saying something for a bloke who was raised on the Reeperbahn.'*

In the end a disgruntled Colonel Schirmer gave up his search, knowing it would be foolish to go any deeper into the jungle, and returned to where the Headhunters, who had now overcome their surprise, were beginning to get ready for the day's march. He gave the order to march out, leaving a section of Spider-arse Kurtz's 1st Company to wait for White Lightning's group to return.

One hour later the 3rd caught up with the column, with Pansy Petersen, his rouged cheeks gleaming with sweat and triumph, pushing a skinny, undersized native, his hands bound behind his back, in front of him. 'Caught him myself, sir,' he announced proudly, as Schirmer ordered the column to halt. 'Nearly fell over him, in fact. I was so surprised that I nearly wet my frillies.' He flipped a limp, bracelet-adorned wrist at Schirmer, who grinned in spite of his angry bewilderment at the strange attack.

He looked down at the prisoner, while Tod hovered at his side in eager anticipation. 'How do you know he's our man, Pansy?' he asked. 'He looks like any other slant-eyed peasant to me.'

'Not just a pretty mug, sir,' the handsome young officer with the rouged cheeks answered. Hastily he untied the sullen man's bonds and ripped down his threadbare blue shirt to reveal a heavy red mark running across his right shoulder and skinny, sunken, yellow chest. 'Obvious, isn't it? He got that from carrying the quiver. Besides smell his hand.'

As if the prisoner were some dumb animal, Pansy Petersen lifted his right hand and thrust it under Schirmer's nose.

*Hamburg's red-light district.

Schirmer sniffed hard and nodded his agreement. 'Cordite smell.'

'Right in one, sir,' Pansy answered cheerfully. 'Got it from firing the star shell.'

'Why you attack us?' Schirmer asked in broken Vietnamese. 'Answer, pig!' His big hand slapped back and forth, sending the prisoner's head slamming from side to side. Just in time White Lightning, his disgust at this type of interrogation obvious, caught him and prevented him from falling.

The 'pig' refused to answer. His dark eyes full of sudden tears and his face sullen, he stared down at his bare feet wordlessly.

Schirmer turned to an expectant Tod, whose eyes were already beginning to gleam with almost sexual excitement behind his gold-rimmed schoolmaster's pince-nez, and snapped, 'All right, Schoolmaster, he's yours. But be quick. I don't want the column stalled on the trail like this very long. It's too dangerous.'

'I shall endeavour to be quick, sir,' Tod purred, eyes only for the prisoner now. 'Clothes off!' he ordered in good Vietnamese.

The prisoner obeyed, taking off his shabby cotton pants and ragged loin-cloth beneath in that same dumb animal manner that seemed to characterise all Vietnamese when they were dealing with the 'round-eyes', as they called their French masters behind their backs.

Tod appraised the man's skinny yellow body with legs like two bean poles, saying, 'Stripping them naked gives them a feeling of being inferior and defenceless, sir. Besides, the Slant-eyes are always shy of physical exposure –'

'Oh, for God's sake, Schoolmaster, get on with it and don't give us a shitting lecture!' Schirmer interrupted angrily.

'*Zu Befehl, Herr Oberst,*' Tod said hastily.

With surprising speed for such a pedantic, considered man, he whipped out his jungle knife and in the same instant yanked back the prisoner's long, greasy black hair to expose his skinny throat. Carefully he drew the needle-sharp point across the skin, drawing blood, saying huskily, 'Did that give you pleasure, prisoner – real pleasure?'

The Slant-eyes did not answer, but his dark eyes, liquid with pain, were testimony enough of what he was feeling at that moment.

The Schoolmaster let go of the prisoner's hair abruptly and began to trace another line of blood across his chest and around his stomach, crooning pleasurably to himself all the time and savouring the look of agony on the Vietnamese's yellow face. Suddenly the knife stopped its bloody progress poised just over the prisoner's sparsely-haired genitals. The chatter among the watching Headhunters died away and suddenly the only sound was the prisoner's gasps of pain and the Schoolmaster's heavy breathing. All eyes were fixed on the blood-tipped point of that cruel knife.

The Schoolmaster took his time, savouring this tremendous moment of power, tiny flecks of foam on his slack lips, his eyes behind the pince-nez gleaming with almost unbearable pleasure. 'Are you going to talk now, prisoner?' he asked in a voice so low and husky that Schirmer and the rest had to strain to catch his question. 'You know, with this knife,' he dug it into the prisoner's skin to emphasize his point and the Vietnamese winced with pain, 'I could operate on you. You wouldn't die, even though I would use no drugs. I am an artist with the knife, you know. Yes, yes, you would live, but you would be only half a man for the rest of your life. Do you know why, prisoner?'

The naked Vietnamese did not answer, but the look in his eyes showed all too clearly that he understood his torturer's intention.

'I shall tell you then, prisoner. Because I . . . I . . .' The Schoolmaster seemed momentarily to have difficulty in controlling his voice. He swallowed hastily and continued, 'because I am going to cut off your testicles if you don't talk. *TALK, OR I'LL SLICE OFF YOUR NUTS!*' he roared in sudden, red-faced fury, splattering the ashen-faced trembling prisoner with spittle.

'Oh, my God!' White Lightning said, sickened at what was to come, and turned away in disgust.

The exclamation distracted the Schoolmaster just as he was lowering the bloody tip of the jungle knife and was preparing to slip it into the prisoner's right testicle. The

Vietnamese flashed out his hand. Before a surprised Tod could stop him, he had grabbed the knife and thrust it deep into his own skinny stomach. Once, twice, three times. His spine tensed and arched from the waist up, his eyes bulged and blood jetted scarlet from the terrible wound, swamping his hand, until he dropped to the ground, jerking convulsively, to die before their shocked eyes . . .

Five minutes later the Headhunters' column was on the march again, heading even deeper into the already sweltering green hell of the jungle, with a puzzled and worried Colonel Schirmer up at point wondering just what Massacre Valley had in store for him and his men.

FOUR

The going was hell!

At point, teams of six men, working for ten minute spells, and gasping for breath like leathern-lunged asthmatics, hacked and carved their way through the jungle for the column, their uniforms black and heavy with sweat, the salt burning their eyes. Giant vines and creepers made their progress slow; the great tendrils caught at their shaking legs and feet and the long, needle-sharp thorns ripped their uniforms and scoured deep red furrows across their naked arms and sweat-lathered, pain-racked faces.

Colonel Schirmer knew how his men must be suffering. But he knew it was safer this way. By abandoning the trail he had reduced the risk of the column being ambushed, and although he kept a wary eye open for booby traps and punji sticks, he thought it hardly likely that the enemy would have penetrated so deep into the jungle to plant them.

Thus they progressed that long afternoon, deep in a green twilit world where the sun scarcely penetrated the high canopy of trees overhead and the heat weighed down upon the toiling men thick and stuffy, wrapping them in a stifling blanket of humidity. Under these conditions, Schirmer knew that they wouldn't make more than 250 metres an hour; but as yet another relieved working party came staggering past him, their limbs trembling with their exertions, their eyes wild and staring on faces dripping with sweat, he told himself this was the only way.

At four o'clock, Schirmer ordered a halt and fresh salt tablets to be issued. While his exhaused Headhunters slumped down gratefully in the little glade, almost too weary to open their canteens for water to wash down the salt tablets and ignoring the insects and stinging flies which descended upon them immediately, Schirmer took

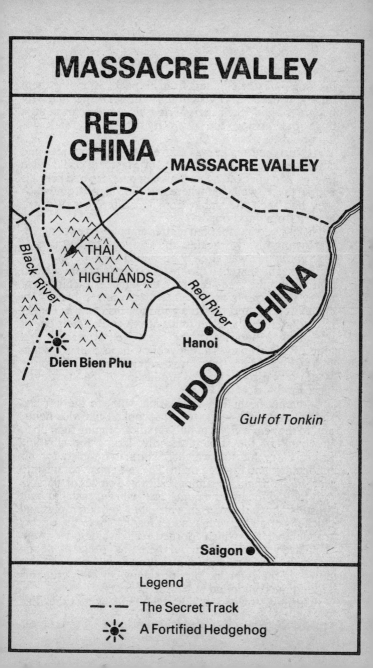

his long-gaff tree climbers from his pack. Strapping them on and with the ever watchful Schulze covering him with his grease-gun, Schirmer started his slow progress up a huge oak, using the deep rivulets in its bark for handholds.

At thirty metres he was above the rest of the trees and could see the dominant peaks of Massacre Valley. He paused and checked against his compass. He had kept his course pretty well, but where was the village from which they had seen the smoke coming on the day they had landed from the choppers?

He climbed another ten metres and paused once again. Narrowing his eyes against the slanting blinding rays of the sun, which was already beginning to go down above the peaks, he searched the area. To the west there seemed nothing but the green carpet of the jungle stretching right up to the mountains. Nowhere was there a break. He clambered around the tree and then his eye was caught immediately by the silver snake of a river. Probably one of the many tributaries of the great Red River, he told himself, his keen eyes already following its course – for in Indo-China where there was water there were people. Water was essential in the production of the Slant-eyes' basic food – rice.

Suddenly he had it. A clearing, with, to the left and right, neat patch-works of what looked like rice-fields, and to the rear a circle of huts on stilts, running right up to the bank of the stream. Hastily, letting the climbing spikes carry his full weight, Schirmer fumbled for his binoculars, and focused them. The settlement sprang into view in the bright, gleaming, calibrated circles of glass.

It looked the usual *montagnard** village, each hut built on stilts above the pens in which they kept their pigs and chickens at night, with a ladder leading up to the rickety wooden balcony which adorned each dwelling. He swept the place with his glasses, but there was no sign of life; no smoke from the chimneys, no half-naked women washing down by the river, no pigs or skinny chickens grubbing around the compound for worms or roots.

Schirmer frowned. If it was the same hamlet they had

*The original inhabitants of Indo-China.

seen from the air, and he was sure it was, what had happened to the inhabitants in the meantime? He cocked his head to one side and listened hard. But there were only the normal sounds of the jungle; those of the birds, the crickets, the cicadas. Old Indo-China hand that he was, Schirmer knew that the absence of jungle noises usually meant danger. How often had he experienced the sudden hush when the enemy was close by; the birds and cicadas would cease their song, leaving behind a tense, noisy silence in which one could hear one's own heart beating excitedly.

Slowly and thoughtfully Schirmer climbed down the oak and reported what he had seen, adding to his attentive officers, 'Gentlemen, we're going to have a look at it. For two reasons. One, it might give us a clue to what is going on up here. Two, if we need to get out of here quick – and I have a nasty feeling in my gut that we might have to – it's the only place the choppers could use as a DZ in the kilometres around.'

White Lightning frowned, worried. 'You're taking a chance, Skipper.'

'The Headhunters always take chances, Major,' Schirmer answered with more confidence than he felt. 'All right, you aspagarus Tarzans, let's get the lead out of our butts!'

'You heard the CO!' Schulze added his bellow to the groans and moans of weary men rising to their feet. '*Haul ass!*'

The terrible march continued.

It was growing dark as the weary column started to move through the fallen trees and piles of jumbled rocks, covered by thorn bushes and vines, that marked the approach to the village. It was still pretty thick and they were making considerable noise so that Schirmer and Shulze up at point were tense and alert, in spite of their tiredness. If anyone was hiding in the riverside settlement, they would have heard them by now. Schirmer in the lead, fatigue and thirst forgotten, could feel that old sense of apprehension, the involuntary tightening of the skin, as the body waited fearfully for the tap-tap of machine-gun fire.

Now they could hear the sound of water running. A second later they could smell it, and the parched sweating Headhunters fought off the almost irresistible urge to run forward and bury their baking faces in the stream. With a hand signal, Schirmer halted the point. He nodded to Schulze. Alone the two of them ventured forward.

The usual jungle sounds. The croak of a bird. A squirrel or tree rat rattling a branch. The slither of a snake through the under-brush. Schirmer paused, cocking his head to one side, ignoring the red ants and the sweat bees which descended upon him instantly. Nothing. Another hand signal and they went on.

The trees started to give out. They began to climb an eroded embankment, marked with the holes of the natives. The settlement must be just over the other side. A twig snapped. The two Headhunters froze instantly, ears cocked and hearts beating like crazy triphammers. Again nothing. Perhaps some jungle animal. Crouching low to make the smallest possible silhouette the two of them rolled over the brow of the embankment and fell flat, weapons raised, ready to fight for their lives. But the expected angry burst of automatic fire did not come.

Down below, next to the stream now glowing a dull scarlet in the rays of the setting sun, the settlement was almost ominously silent. Schirmer issued a hurried order over his walkie-talkie, then nodded to Schulze. Gripping their grease-guns tightly in sweating hands, they approached the hamlet. While Schulze covered him, Schirmer crept cautiously up the rickety ladder of the first stilt-house.

Experience had taught him that there were various ways of entering the native house. But one you never used if you wished to live – straight through the doorway, as if one were passing through the door of some village house back in the Fatherland. Instead, Schirmer aimed a tremendous kick at the door, sending it flying open, in the same instant that he jumped to one side to flatten himself against the wall, grease-gun at the ready.

The first hut was empty, as were all the others the two Headhunters examined. All the evidence, however, was that they had been abandoned hastily. Why else, Schirmer reasoned, would the *montagnards* have left behind their cooking pots on the rotting wooden floors and, in one case, nearly half a sack of precious rice?

A parched, puzzled Schulze, his kepi thrust to the back of his big blond head, commented as they stood there in the middle of the abandoned compound, 'Colonel, I don't know what you feel like, but Mrs Schulze's handsome son can already feel the crap begin to trickle down his leg. Something's up here, and Schulze don't like it one bit!'

Schirmer could do nothing but agree with him.

'*Sir . . .sir . . .*'

Schirmer spun round from his Officer Group, which he was holding in the middle of the compound before the men settled down for the night.

A pale-faced bareheaded young Headhunter was running awkwardly towards him, holding up his trousers with one hand and waving excitedly with the other, his eyes threatening, so it seemed, to pop out of his head at any moment.

'Oooo, la, la,' Pansy Petersen commented delightedly. 'I just wonder what he's been up to, the naughty boy.'

'Knock it off, Pansy!' White Lightning snapped, realising at once that the man running towards them had just suffered a shock. He dashed forward and grabbed the terror-stricken soldier by the arm, halting him. 'What is it, man?' he demanded.

The man stared at him wild-eyed, his lower lip trembling violently. 'Everywhere,' he quavered, his eyes rolling. 'They're every – '

His words ended in a sudden gasp of pain, as White Lightning smacked him smartly across his pale young face. 'Pull yourself together,' he barked. 'Remember you're in the Legion!'

For a moment the boy looked as if he were going to cry, then he felt his reddening cheeks tenderly and said in a broken voice, 'I was going to have a crap outside the village . . . I don't like to shit in the thunderbox with all the rest – '

'Get on with it!'

'Well, I thought I'd found a good quiet place and had just squatted down when I saw it.' His face paled again alarmingly at the thought.

'Saw what?' Schirmer snapped.

'The hand . . . the hand protruding from the earth – '

'*Come on*!' Schirmer bellowed, foregoing the rest of the explanation.

All weariness gone now, the officers doubled across the compound, pushing aside the astonished Headhunters, and headed in the direction indicated by the shocked young trooper. Schirmer saw it and skidded to a stop. Just to the right of the pile of paper and an abandoned machine-pistol which marked the spot where the soldier had squatted down was a hand in the freshly disturbed earth – *and it was white*!

With the sudden clarity of a vision, Colonel Erwin Schirmer knew that they had found one of the missing strike battalions. His voice tired and without emotion, he said, without looking round at his abruptly halted officers, 'Get a work party up here – with spades, will you?'

FIVE

'But why?' Schirmer asked, breaking the heavy silence engendered by the shocking discovery, as the Headhunters' officers squatted in the compound, heating canteen cups of coffee over the hissing fire made of plastic explosive. 'Why bury them in the first place?'

Schirmer shivered a little at the mental picture of those four hundred bodies they had discovered just beneath the surface of the field behind the settlement, ripped and torn by explosive bullets and many of them mutilated after death; their eyes gouged out, fingers hacked off, and with in some cases the genitals excised and placed mockingly between the gaping lips.

Spider-arse, named thus because of his strange gait, the result of the damage caused by an explosive shell in his right buttock at Stalingrad in '42, blew at the steaming hot coffee and said, 'Yes, usually Uncle Ho's boys throw them on the nearest shit-heap and let their pigs feed their fill on the corpses. Do you think they're getting soft in their old age?'

'I doubt it. Not those perverted banana-suckers,' Thiel growled, his voice slurred a little from the litre of cognac he had already drunk that evening. 'We Round-eyes are not worth a spadeful o' dirt to those yeller heathens.'

White Lightning, his face hollowed out to a death's head in the flickering blue light of the burning explosive, said slowly, 'I've been thinking about it ever since we found the stiffs, Skipper, and I think I've come up with the answer.'

The weary Headhunter officers turned their gazes in the hairless American's direction curiously.

White Lightning continued to stare into the fire. Outside the camp there was no sound save the soft pad-pad of a patrolling sentry and the howl of some night creature in the jungle beyond the stream.

'Well?' Schirmer said when the American did not speak. 'What is your theory? I'll be glad of some light on the subject, for I must confess I don't know what to make of the events of the last forty-eight hours.'

'One,' the American said, ticking the numeral off on his fingers, 'Uncle Ho doesn't want trouble. They'd spotted us right from the start, but they didn't do anything even while we were landing, the most critical phase of a DZ op. Two, my guess is that he thought that the arrow business would be enough to frighten us off, as it might have done the average Frog outfit. Three, the CO of those poor dead guys out there must have pressed home his sweep and forced Uncle Ho to show his hand. But afterwards he took good care to hide the stiffs so that they couldn't be spotted by air recon.'

'But why?' Schirmer persisted. 'Why all the fuss? They've been killing Frogs for eight years or more now – why go to lengths like that?'

'I don't know, Skipper,' White Lightning said plaintively. 'All I know is that they haven't deterred us, made us turn back and get out of this damned valley.'

Next to him 'Pansy' Petersen, holder of the Knight's Cross and the Golden Wound Badge,* shivered and, throwing an apprehensive look over his shoulder as if he imagined Uncle Ho might be standing right behind him, quavered, 'I say, Ami, don't say things like that or I'll have to ask one of those young virgins of mine to sleep with me tonight, I'm so scared.'

But for once no one laughed at the homosexual's outrageous remarks; they were all too preoccupied with the implications of White Lightning's last remark.

Finally Schirmer broke the heavy silence and put what they were all thinking into words, 'Schulze,' he commanded. 'See that the sentries are doubled tonight – and Kurtz, your company better stand to just before dawn.'

Kurtz nodded his agreement, draining the last of his coffee and rising to his feet. 'Yes, Colonel, that *is* the time when they're likely to attack. Good night, sir . . .'

---

*Granted to a soldier wounded six or more times in battle.

'I say we must attack them, Comrade Ho!' General Giap said fiercely, his broad yellow face set and his prominent eyes bulging angrily as he stamped across the earthen floor of his command post. Outside the coolies toiled in the dust.

Ho-Chi-Minh stroked his wispy grey goatee and told himself that Giap was in one of his 'great captain' moods. The ex-teacher of history was always very concerned with his military prestige and his place in posterity; he was given to impetuous, boldly Napoleonic decisions which often did not go well with the human resources at his disposal.

'I must admit, Comrade General, that the appearance of the enemy in the Thai Mountains at this time is tiresome, but perhaps we should not take it too seriously.'

Giap swung round and stared at 'He-Who-Lights-The-Way', as the leader of the Vietnamese revolution was now calling himself, as if he were seeing him for the first time. 'We cannot take a simple chance *now*, comrade,' he barked. 'All these months of preparation, all the work,' he pointed out of the glassless window at the Red Highway, where the barefoot coolies toiled by the flaring light of pine torches while a fresh group of supply men with their grossly overladen, camouflaged cycles waited to continue south. 'Nothing must be risked now, Comrade Ho.'

'Comrade Mao says in his *Ten Commandments* that one should fight no engagements in which there is no assurance of victory,' Ho said softly, expressing yet again his doubts about Giap's bold plan.

'I know, Comrade. Did I not sit at the Great Mao's feet myself in China ten years ago? But there will be victory this time – a great victory. My plan is, as you well know, to let the French believe that they are winning. I don't want to stir up any trouble until we are ready to strike. Out there is my secret weapon. Nothing must endanger it, comrade.'

He flung out his right hand dramatically at the Red Highway, which was being carved through the jungle by the thousands of toiling coolies, with overhead the crowns of the trees drawn together by ropes and pullies to prevent it being seen from the air. 'Once it is completed, then I shall strike – and strike tremendously hard.'

Giap thrust out his heavy jaw, as if he were posing for a portrait painting of the Soviet realist school, Ho couldn't help thinking.

'All right, Comrade General, I agree to the attack on these new French intruders. But there must be no survivors and no warning to the French HQ.'

'There will be none,' Giap replied, beaming now that he had won his point. 'I am sending in the Death Volunteers.'

Abruptly Uncle Ho shivered violently at the memory of that terribly mutilated face. 'Captain Napalm's men?' he asked hoarsely.

'Exactly, Napalm's Death Volunteers,' Giap answered savouring the words. 'There will be no escape – *from them*!'

SIX

It was nearly dawn now.

The moon was beginning to wane. Gradually the calls and cries of the night creatures were beginning to recede into the remote distance. The pre-dawn hush was descending upon the thick black mass of the jungle, broken only by the ripple of the stream, which still shone a dull silver in the fading moonlight.

Schulze, standing next to Schirmer and Lieutenant Kurtz, yawned wearily and rubbed eyes that felt as if they were filled with grains of coarse sand. 'What a shitting life!' he exclaimed without rancour. 'Up at this hour in the middle of shittingly well nowhere! Ought to have my shitting head examined!'

Kurtz laughed hollowly, a strange sound at that time of day. 'Who else would have you, you big rogue?' he said. 'You know you have to work in the big world outside.'

Schulze groaned mournfully. 'Don't mention work, Lieutenant. Ain't things bad enough as they are?'

Schirmer remained silent. What were they doing here, he asked himself, prompted by Schulze's tired comment, German soldiers fighting a French war for an empire in which they played no part, against natives whose cause presented no danger to them? Eight weary long years they had been at it now – for what?

Schirmer dismissed the questions. Didn't all soldiers ask the same thing in the small hours of the morning when the lonely or bored mind was given to such introspection? They were here because they were here; because they were the Legion's Headhunters, whose only homeland now was that of the Legion. His mind blank, the big colonel wandered on with the other two along the alert company's riverside positions, while the rest of the Headhunters snored away happily, lost in the soldier's pathetic little dreams of wine and women.

'Give it another fifteen, twenty minutes and it'll be first light,' Schulze commented. 'The cooks'll be able to get some nigger sweat going then. I could do with a sip of something hot – my tonsils are as dried up as a retired slit on the *Reeperbahn*.'

Kurtz paused and, pushing back his kepi, surveyed the dull silver of the river, with the dark outline of a log or something similar floating down it slowly. 'Yer, I'll be glad to stand the men down. These pre-dawn stand-tos take it out of you when you've got a long march ahead of you the next morning.'

'Surprised to hear you say such things, Lieutenant,' Schulze said in his best officer-and-gentleman's voice. 'You know that – '

WHIIIZZ!

The sudden frightening hush froze the rest of his words on his lips.

'*Look out, Kurtz*!' Schirmer screamed.

Too late! The arrow tore through the thickets and slammed directly into the officer's chest. He screamed once and fell sideways, thrashing in agony in a flurry of dirt and leaves.

The dying officer's company reacted almost immediately, as a second and third barbed arrow came winging in from the direction of the river. Rifles cracked, grease-guns hushed, machine-guns chattered frantically, sending a burning stream of white tracer hissing angrily across the sudden glowing surface of the water. Branches cracked and broke. Leaves came raining down in green profusion, and on the log floating by, a thin arm was raised in noiseless agony before the dead body slid into the water and was washed slowly ashore as the frenetic chatter died away, leaving behind it a low, echoing, frightening silence.

Schirmer lowered Kurtz's head gently to the ground and then as an afterthought closed both eyelides with his thumb

'Bought it, sir?' Schulze asked.

Schirmer nodded wordlessly and, rising, walked over to where the dead sniper was nudging back and forth against the mud bank, while all around the suddenly very alert Headhunters stared intently into the dirty white pre-dawn gloom. Behind them there were the sounds of the camp waking up quickly.

Disdainfully, using the toe of his boot as if he were touching a very dirty object, Schulze turned over the half-naked body of the dead youth, clad only in a wet loincloth and a black bandage or turban wrapped around his head. Slowly, as if possessed by a life of its own, the grey-green snake of the dead youth's intestines started to crawl out of his shattered guts. But Schirmer had no eyes for the terrible wound. His gaze was fixed on the crudely tattooed skull-and-crossbones which adorned the centre of the youth's brow beneath the black bandage. 'You know what that means, don't you, Schulze?' he asked, his voice toneless.

Schulze whistled softly through his front teeth and cursed, 'Great shit on the shingle. *Death Volunteers*! Now we really are in for a packet!'

'That indeed we are,' Schirmer agreed, staring down at the dead member of Uncle Ho's most feared and élite troops, who had all sworn an oath to take their objective or die. Whenever they attacked, either they were victorious or they didn't come back to attempt to explain their failure.

Suddenly he snapped out of the strange lethargy engendered by the surprise killing. 'Stand to, everywhere,' he yelled at the top of his voice. *'STAND TO . . . AT THE DOUBLE NOW . . . WE'RE UNDER ATTACK, HEADHUNTERS!'*

Colonel Schirmer wiped a bead of stinking sweat from his face and stared angrily at the impenetrable belt of green jungle. 'Old trick, Major,' he said to White Lightning crouching next to him in the foxhole. 'War of nerves.'

'Yeah, they're setting us up,' the hairless American agreed. 'Listen, there they go again.' He cocked his head in the direction of the jungle tiger's roar. 'And it's not even halfway like the real thing. But I suppose they think it'll get on our nerves, just like that business with the arrow.'

'Agreed. The Death Volunteers might be Uncle Ho's kamikazies but obviously they're not going to throw away their lives heedlessly. They want a maximum return for their deaths.'

'But what are they trying to achieve?' he asked as the obvious click of a rifle bolt being drawn back across the water indicated another stage in their war of nerves with the unseen assailants. 'I mean – Je-sus – what good is one archer against a whole battalion of the Legion?'

'Good job we are the Legion. If we'd have been ordinary legs, we would have sent out a patrol and walked straight into the little ambush they have got set up for us somewhere out there.' Schirmer frowned hard, feeling the hot rays of the sun burn through his shirt and sear the skin below. 'No, Major, we've got to stick it out *here*, in spite of all their tricks. Sooner or later, they're going to attack,' he slapped the butt of his grease-gun angrily, 'and then we're going to give those damned Slant-eyes a very warm reception.'

'You can say that again, Skipper,' White Lightning agreed.

Time passed leadenly, with the Headhunters baking in their holes, limited by Schirmer's order to a sip of water an hour; he didn't want his men falling to the snipers who would now be watching the stream for anyone attempting to take water from it. Twice a sudden flurry of noise, such as that of many hurrying feet, had altered the sweating, lethargic men and had set their strained nerves tingling, but nothing had come of the supposed attack and the apparent rush had died away as quickly as it had come. Once, too, a star shell had exploded directly above the compound, bathing their tense, upturned faces a bloody hue. Again, nothing had materialised. It was all part of the cat-and-mouse game the Death Volunteers were playing with them. To Schirmer, crouched next to the sweat-drenched, stinking White Lightning and Schulze in their foxhole, it seemed as if he could almost hear the minutes of their tense, nerve-racking vigil tick away.

By midday, with the sun's glare cutting their eyes like the blade of a sharp knife and its rays roasting their unprotected backs so that their bodies streamed with sweat, attracting insidious flies and insects, Colonel Schirmer had had enough. Angrily he told himself he was letting the enemy dictate to him how the coming battle should be conducted.

'Schulze,' he barked.

'Sir.'

'Put your kepi on the end of your grease-gun. When I give the order raise it, and keep your big turnip down.'

'Don't worry about me, sir,' Schulze answered cheerfully enough, in spite of the fact that his shirt was black with sweat, with great, dried salt rings under the armpits. 'Ain't a Slant-eyes born yet who could put one over on Mrs Schulze's handsome lad.'

'Get on with it!' Schirmer snapped impatiently.

Cautiously Schulze raised his cap, while Schirmer tensed for action. It came. *Crack*! There was a brisk snap like that of a dry twig cracking under foot. Schulze reeled back, yelping with pain, his grease-gun trembling in his smarting hand, a neat hole drilled through his kepi.

Schirmer pressed his trigger. The grease-gun hissed. Lead splattered the tree top from which the shot had come. Its branches parted and tore. Slowly a skinny brown body tumbled from the tree top and hit the stream below with a great silver splash of suddenly disturbed water.

'Cheer!' Schirmer cried loudly. 'Cheer, for Christ sake! Get the Slant-eyes rattled.'

A hoarse cheer broke out all along the perimeter, swelling in strength and continuing long after the sound of Schirmer's burst had died away. For the first time that long morning Schirmer grinned. He could almost sense just how angry his unseen opponents were.

'All right,' he commanded five minutes later, knowing that the Death Volunteers would not fall for the same old trick twice but aware that he must keep up his own war-of-nerves if he was to get them to make the first move, 'let's give them the *Boudin*. One, two, *three*!'

The rough, untrained voices of the Headhunters burst into the Foreign Legion's song, one which legionnaires had chanted for over 120 years from Mexico to Papeete and one which was like a red rag to the Slant-eyes, who hated the Legion. With all the strength of their enraged frustration drowning the jungle noises, they bellowed the verses in German:

Mein Regiment, mein Heimatland
Meine Mutter hab' ich nie gekannt
Mein Vater starb schon frueh in Feld.
Ich bin allein auf dieser Welt.*

Schirmer could feel tangibly how his opponents' rage was beginning to grow as that great song swept over their positions, strong, confident and proud, challenging them to take some action.

'Now the *Horst Wessel*,' he commanded after the last verse of the *Boudin* had died away.

Obediently his Headhunters smashed into the marching song of the stormtroopers, bringing back memories of their proud swagger down the cobbled streets of the Reich, their steel-helmeted bodies rigid, their steel-tipped jackboots crashing down on the stone.

'The old *Wotan* marching song!' Schulze cried, carried away by the rising tension, aware like his CO that the growing volume of noise in the jungle across the stream indicated that something was going to happen soon – and very soon.

Blood is our beer, steel our meat
Nothing we fear, we know no defeat . . .

The bold words echoed and re-echoed across the water.

Better dead than red . . . SS Assault Battalion Wotan
march – enemy ahead . . .

Abruptly the last verse was drowned by an obscene howl, which tore the air apart with a frightening, ear-splitting roar.

'Incoming mail!' White Lightning yelled as the first mortar bombs plopped down in the river, sending huge spurts of angry, boiling white water into the blazing sky.

Just in time Schirmer cowered at the bottom of his pit as the enemy mortar fire submerged the Headhunters' positions, showering his back with earth, twigs and splinters.

*My regiment is my home. My mother I never knew. My father died in battle. I am alone in this world.

His plan had worked. The Death Volunteers had made the first move, and yet even at this moment of minor triumph, a puzzled little voice inside his head asked, *And how in hell's name did the Slant-eyes get 81mm mortars this far into the mountains*?

Even that overwhelming question of logistics was soon forgotten as the earth rose and swayed beneath him like a live thing and the Death Volunteers' softening-up barrage rose to its terrifying crescendo. Soon – very soon now – they would be coming across the river.

SEVEN

'*Xung Phong*!' the shrill cry rose all along the opposite river bank.

'*Here they come*!' someone cried excitedly.

'*Stand to . . . stand to*!' Whistles shrilled. NCOs bellowed orders. Officers rapped into their walkie-talkies.

'*STAND TO*!'

The Death Volunteers burst from the trees, waving their black banners and screaming hoarsely with bugles and trumpets blaring. They hit the water in a rush of wild white foam.

At once the Headhunters' line erupted with fire. Scarlet flashes crackled along the whole line. Tracer zipped flatly over the water, dragging glowing, deadly shadows behind it. The leading Volunteers went down by the dozen, threshing the water to a bloody foam in their dying agonies, as their comrades came splashing and blundering by them, knowing with desperate fury that they were sitting ducks as long as they remained in the river. They scrambled fervently for the opposite bank.

'Grenades!' Schirmer bellowed over the snap and crackle of the murderous fire fight, slinging his grease-gun and snatching the grenade clipped to his webbing. With a quick bite, he had pulled out the pin, spat it out and flung the round ball of lethal explosive in one smooth movement. It exploded just in front of the bearer of the black flag. He stopped as if he had just run into a brick wall. Suddenly his head disintegrated in a flash of scarlet, bloody gore. His flag dropped into the blood-red water, as if to signify the end of the Death Volunteers' first suicidal attack. But as the Headhunters' grenades hastened the survivors of that wild charge back to their start positions, a suddenly weak, weary Schirmer realised they would be back – and soon.

They came from the right flank. This time there were no warcries and no banners. They came like black jungle snakes, slithering from boulder to boulder, using every bit of cover like the veterans they were and getting as close as they could to the corrugated ridge behind the compound.

White Lightning watched them come, calm and detached, almost as if he were viewing a newsreel in some local movie theatre; he was unmoved also by the obvious nervousness of his Headhunters, who were worried now that the Death Volunteers were getting so close.

'Take it easy,' he whispered softly at regular intervals. 'Take it easy . . . But when I order fire, give them the works, the whole goddam works!' As if to emphasize just how calm he himself was, he lit a cheroot and crouched there, puffing away at the black cigar contentedly.

The first of the Death Volunteers reached the edge of the ridge, naked and bare of trees, its side corrugated and furrowed like the back of some ancient crocodile. They hesitated among the boulders, perhaps even their legendary courage faltering at the thought of advancing onto the bare steep slope. The first skinny, barefoot figure detached itself from the cover and approached the ridge. White Lightning snapped an urgent order. The corporal who had raised his grease-gun dropped it again, chastened. White Lightning continued to puff at his cheroot. The single barefoot Volunteer started to toil up the naked ridge. Another followed – and another.

Within seconds the whole ridge seemed covered by their black, toiling figures. Still White Lightning did not move. All around him the Headhunters began to breathe more shallowly, the air coming in short, sharp gasps, as if they were preparing to run a race. Now there were half a hundred of the Death Volunteers on the rock face less than a hundred metres away. White Lightning savoured his cigar.

Seventy-five metres! There was a whole company of them on the ridge now, scrambling upwards nimbly, eager to reach the top and have it over with.

Fifty metres! The tense, ashen-faced Headhunters staring down the length of their weapons could see the Volunteers' faces – stark, yellow, set, with teeth drawn back from bared lips – loom up ever larger in the round metal circle of their sights. *When* would the Major order them to fire?

Thirty metres! In a minute the Volunteers would be at the top of the ridge and would charge all-out, rushing the Headhunter positions at the point of the bayonet.

Twenty-five metres! It was now or never!

Abruptly, White Lightning rose to his feet. In full view of the attackers, he tossed aside his cheroot with dramatic suddenness. Raising his grease-gun and taking quick aim, he screamed, '*FIRE*!'

Half a hundred automatics burst into action. The murderous stream of lead swept the leading Volunteers from the rock-face in bloody, howling, crazy profusion, leaving a handful of unwounded to slither down into the second wave, their nails ripped off and hands streaming blood and dust.

'*Loose fire*!' White Lightning screamed. 'Pick your own targets, men! Give 'em hell!'

The Headhunters needed no urging. All tension released now, their strained, sweating faces set in wolfish grins of sadistic pleasure, they snapped burst after burst at the Volunteers trapped on the slope. The second line was scythed away. Behind them the third line, howling like crazy men, kept on coming; even with ever greater holes in their ranks, they still kept on coming.

White Lightning pelted forward to where the first of the enemy was tumbling over the edge of the ridge. He fired off a burst. A Vietnamese went down screaming, his face sawn off. Another came racing at the American. He pressed his trigger. Nothing! Either he had emptied the magazine or there was a stoppage. The little yellow man screamed with triumph. Not for long. White Lightning's heavy boot shot up. It connected with the Volunteer's crotch. He fell writhing to the ground, his scream drowned in vomit. Next instant the butt of White Lightning's grease-gun smashed down on his upturned, agonized, yellow face cruelly. Bones splintered. Thick red blood jetted up from his nostrils and mouth and mingled with the suddenly brilliant white of broken teeth.

Now the Volunteers were everywhere among the handful of Headhunters holding the ridge. There was no room for manoeuvre. It was every man for himself. Knives and bayonets flashed. Shovels slashed. Men, white and yellow, swayed back and forth, locked in an embrace of death. Below their feet the dead and dying were trampled upon cruelly. No quarter was given or expected. It was a battle to the death.

White Lightning grabbed the bayonet of the fallen Volunteer. Just in time. Another came rushing at him, bayonet at the ready. Their weapons locked. With a twist of his wrist and a heave of his right thigh, he smashed the Volunteer's bayonet to one side. The man staggered back. White Lightning drove his blade home, deep into the Vietnamese's guts, right up to the muzzle. For one long moment the two of them stood there transfixed, the crumpled figure of the Volunteer, death already filling his popping eyes, supported by White Lightning's blade. Then the American aimed a savage kick at his guts and the bayonet came free with a horrifying, sucking noise. The dead man crumpled to the body-littered ground.

Another Volunteer charged the panting, blood-bespattered American, howling as if demented. He lifted his bayonet to thrust home its half-metre long, needle-sharp blade. White Lightning beat him to it. He parried. The Vietnamese thrust again. The American ducked and yelped with pain as the bayonet gouged a long piece of flesh from his shoulder. Red-enraged lights flashing before his eyes, he stuck his own bayonet forward. The Vietnamese half-turned. Too late. The blade ripped along the length of his naked sunken chest. He howled with pain and dropped his bayonet.

White Lightning didn't hesitate. He brought up the brass-bound butt of the rifle and smashed it savagely into the man's gaping mouth. He sank down on his knees at the edge of the ridge, spitting blood and teeth. White Lightning jerked back the trigger. The rifle spoke. The back of the Volunteer's skull exploding in a gory spray of scarlet blood and broken bone tissue. Without a single sound, he flew over the edge of the ridge, sailing effortlessly high and out into the air, to smash to the ground far below like a broken, abandoned, yellow doll.

'*Hit the dirt*!' It was Pansy Petersen. '*Hit the dirt, you perverted banana-suckers*!'

Instinctively what was left of the defenders dropped to

the ground, leaving their attackers towering above them
in triumph. But not for long. As the Volunteers came in
for the kill, the massed machine-guns of the relieving
company whirled into action, erupting from behind the
boulders only fifty metres away. White Lightning buried
his face in the warm earth as the slugs zipped hotly above
his soaked back, tugging at his shirt, to slam right into the
Vietnamese.

Everywhere the Volunteers collapsed in heaps of
agonized, bloody flesh. Staggering under the impact of
that tremendous salvo at such close range, they seemed
simply to melt away, littering the ground with what appeared to be a scarlet carpet of heaving human tissue.

Moments later, Pansy was shaking White Lightning,
who still had his face buried in the dirt, by the shoulder,
'Come, come now, Major, we mustn't play hide-and-seek
any longer. The nasty men have gone away.' He beamed
down at White Lightning paternally. But even as he said
the words, the blare of bugles and the shrill screams of
charging men indicated that the Death Volunteers were
attacking again.

'*Xung Phong*!' The Death Volunteers' battle-cry rang out
as they entered the water at the bend, which concealed
the crossing point from the defenders. 'Forward
. . . KILL!'

'*A la baionnette*!' Colonel Schirmer yelled, suddenly
alarmingly aware of the danger that was coming from his
left river flank. There was the ominous slither of steel
being slipped out of metal scabbards and the ringing click
of the blades being attached. Anxiously Schirmer waited
till his Headhunters were finished, the noise of the enemy
splashing through the shallows beyond the palms getting
ever louder. 'Form a skirmish line!' he commanded.

'Come on . . . come on, you soft pricks!' Schulze bellowed, his broad face crimson as if with rage, level-
ling angry kicks at laggards. 'Get some tail-wind up
there!'

Schirmer flung one last glance at the thin line of sweating, anxious men and then turned to face his front, from
which the cries and screams of the Volunteers echoed

frighteningly. 'Headhunters,' he cried at the top of his voice, 'At the double – *charge!*'

Carried away by that melodramatic command and the nerve-tingling, hypnotic blood-lust of battle, all fear forgotten now, the lean, blond men doubled forward, springing over fallen trees and smashing through bushes, not heeding the thorns ripping at their clothes and flesh, their wide-eyed gazes intent on the first sight of the enemy. When they were through the bushes, there they were – half a hundred Volunteers – splashing and blundering through the river, already halfway across.

'*FI-RE!*' Schirmer screamed.

The skirmish line skidded to a halt. Chests heaving with the effort and limbs trembling with exertion, fear and rage, the Headhunters loosed a volley from the hip. The leading Volunteers seemed to halt in the middle of their clumsy rush. For one long dramatic moment nothing appeared to happen, and then abruptly they were falling everywhere, screaming, hands raised high as if in supplication, as they disappeared below the surface of the blood-churned water.

'At them!' Schirmer yelled above the drowning screams of the Vietnamese. '*ALLES FUER DEUTSCHLAND!*'

'*ALLES FUER DEUTSCHLAND!*' his Headhunters roared back in one hoarse bellow, and then they were pelting into the water to run slap into the confused attackers.

Schulze lunged forward with his bayoneted grease-gun. The tall Volunteer avoided his thrust easily. Carried forward by the impetus, the big ex-docker nearly fell on his face in the water.

The Vietnamese, who had lost his weapon, grabbed hold of Schulze with his dripping hands. Schulze's nostrils were suddenly assailed by the stench of the rotten fish-paste sauce. 'Get yer evil flippers off me!' he bellowed with rage, as the other man tightened his grip.

The Volunteer squeezed at the big man's neck. Schulze dropped his useless grease-gun in the water. He thrust up his right hand, the heel of the palm extended outwards. The Vietnamese dodged the blow easily.

'Slant-eyed barnshitter!' Schulze gasped as the stars started to explode in front of his eyes and his lungs seemed

to be about to burst at any moment. Desperately he
sought and found the Vietnamese's genitals. With all his
strength he squeezed them. The Volunteer screamed with
agony. That vice-like grip on Schulze's neck was released.

Gasping for breath as the Vietnamese doubled up,
retching and vomiting, Schulze snapped up his right arm,
thrust it behind his back and ducked his head deep into
the water. The Vietnamese's gasps ended abruptly in a
series of violent bubbles. Frantically he tried to lash out
with his right boot. Schulze avoided the blow easily. Ignoring the savage mêlée going on in the shallows all
around him, Schulze held on to his opponent. The
trapped man threshed the water white. Schulze forced the
man's head deeper and deeper, his own boots grinding on
the smooth pebbles below as he fought to retain his
balance and his lips bared to reveal savagely gritted teeth.

'*Won't you ever shittingly well croak*?' Schulze gasped
as the Vietnamese continued to thresh and slap the water
in his dying torment, and then finally he gave up the ghost.
After one last desperate twist from Schulze's big wet
hands dug deep into the skinny neck, holding on for all he
was worth, suddenly the Vietnamese went limp.

Slowly Schulze relaxed his grip. The body rose to the
surface and floated there, face downwards, the mop of
coal-black hair spreading out like a seaborne wreath,
while Schulze sat down in the water, oblivious to the
splashing hurrying feet all around him and the mingled
cries of triumph and enraged panic, which indicated that
the river attack had failed, too, and the Volunteers were
withdrawing yet again.

Captain Napalm stood motionlessly on the little hillock
overlooking the river, accompanied only by his bugler,
watching the survivors come streaming back, wading
through the dead floating on the surface of the pink-
tinged water, their eyes round with shock and their
mouths gasping from the effort. Calmly he accepted the
fact that his third attack had failed and he had lost over
two companies. But he had another four companies of
Death Volunteers hidden in the jungle behind him, already chewing the opiates which made them impervious

to fear, ready to rush to their deaths – even eager and happy to do so.

'Victory, Comrade Commander,' a soaked Volunteer gasped, the white blur of his lung moving in and out in the bloody hole in his skinny chest. He raised his clenched right fist as he staggered by.

'Victory, comrade,' Captain Napalm said huskily from behind the black silk mask which covered his face, and he half-raised the terribly burnt right arm, which hung from his side like a black withered branch.

Captain Napalm's hooded eyes searched the landscape with its shattered trees about the shell-churned mud, with the mutilated dead lying everywhere on the bank and in the bloody water, as if some mad surgeon had gone to work with explosives instead of a scalpel. 'Would the French attempt to counter-attack?' he asked himself. He decided they wouldn't. In Indo-China they still retained the Maginot Line mentality of their own far-off country, which he had once loved, even after he had begun to fight against them until – . He continued that terrible thought no further. After *those* terrible five minutes, he had loved no one any more. Thereafter he had only hated. Everybody! No, the French would not attack. But he would – once it grew dark – coming in from both flanks.

He turned to the bugler and said in that strange, huskily sibilant hiss of his, 'Bugler – sound the general retreat.'

'Yes, Comrade Captain.'

The bugler raised his brass trumpet to his lips. It was in that same instant that a faint breeze raised the black silk mask that covered the tall, emaciated commander's face. The young bugler shivered at the sight. The skull was squeezed almost flat and ran to a point, with two great bulging eyes that peered out from what looked like a mass of scarlet, congealed lava, in which no human feature was discernible – not the nose, mouth or cheekbones – save for the twin scarlet pits of the nostrils from which oozed a thick, opaque mucus. Now the boy knew why they called the commander of the Death Volunteers *Captain Napalm* . . .

EIGHT

It was growing dark now. Dark shadows were coming down from the mountains and slipping in evil silence into the jungle. In the compound there was little sound save for the soft moans of the wounded and the steady chop-chop of the fatigue-men, getting the logs ready as commanded.

Schirmer tossed away the last of his cigarette and stared around at the dirty, sweaty-stained but expectant faces of his officers. 'All right,' he commenced, 'I don't have to explain to you what will happen tonight.'

'Standard-operating-procedure,' White Lightning did the work for him. 'As soon as it's dark enough, they'll start infiltrating our forward positions. Thereafter, a mortar barrage to make us keep our heads down, and then the usual bum's rush from three sides.'

'Exactly, Major. More likely than not, they're already moving up the lead parties. So what are we going to do?'

'Dig a shitting big hole and hide in it?' Pansy Petersen, a blood-stained scarf wrapped around his head dramatically, said in his usual flippant manner.

'Fraid it just wouldn't be big enough for all of us, Pansy,' Schirmer said.

'Well, one thing is for sure,' Thiel said, sipping his flask of cognac, 'we've got to get out of here somehow or other before they bring up the rest of the red hordes. Then we wouldn't stand a shitting chance in hell.'

'Agreed,' Schirmer picked up a twig and sketched in their positions hastily in the dust. 'As you know they're all around us – here, here and here. The most thinly covered spot is here on the ridge. But if we were spotted on that, it would be suicide, just as they found out to *their* cost this afternoon.'

'Brother, that you can say again,' White Lightning commented, thinking again of that bloody slaughter on the rocks. 'The shit really did hit the fan!'

'Usual tactic, sir,' Pansy suggested, serious now. 'Hit them where they least expect it. Here,' he reached over and pointed to the river line. 'They won't expect us to attack over the water. They'd think we'd make too much noise, but if – '

'There's going to be no attack,' Schirmer interrupted him softly. 'We've lost too many men already and we can't afford any more casualties. You see, gentlemen, a vague idea is beginning to form in my head. We've really hit on something – something very important in this damned valley.'

'What do you mean, sir?' Pansy asked.

'Well, those mortars they used – they're 81mms, if I'm not mistaken, of Chinese or American manufacture. Now how in three devils' name did they lug those monsters through the jungle all the way from the Chink frontier?' He stared around their tired, unshaven faces, but none of them had any answers.

'Then this business with the Death Volunteers. There must be at least a reinforced battalion out there. Why send a whole battalion of their best troops into open warfare when they usually employ them in small-group commando-type ops, and why let them take the kind of casualties they took today? For all Uncle Ho knows, we are just another routine Frog sweep. Why waste his best Slope-heads on us?' Schirmer licked his cracked lips and stared down at the river over which the first lazy grey coils of the night fog were beginning to uncurl. 'And then there is the business of those buried Frogs of the strike battalion.' He shook his shaven head. 'No, gentlemen, something strange is going on here and I intend to find out what it is.'

Thiel took a swig of his cognac, as if he needed it before he asked his question. 'Well, sir, if we're going to break out without attacking the slant-eyed shits, what are we to do then?'

Schirmer hesitated for only a fraction of a second. Then he made his decision. 'This. . . .'

The crickets had fallen silent at last. Over the surface of the river a thin mist writhed eerily, shrouding the dead who lay sprawled like abandoned bundles of rags all along the mud bank. All was quiet save for the slither of what might have been some jungle animal crawling through the undergrowth busy on some nocturnal hunt.

The gaunt, masked figure standing at the bank in the thick shadow cast by a tree knew differently. The vague slithering sound was made by his Volunteers crawling into position, preparing for the final attack, which would sweep the French from the compound. Now his men were almost ready. He narrowed his eyes and stared out through the slits in the mask at the 81mm mortars, dug in along the bank. In thirty minutes he would order them to open up. Six sharp swift rounds per barrel to soften up the French and make them keep their heads down and then they would attack.

For a moment he stared at the soft beauty of the mist curling and uncurling over the surface of water, in which floated black, rigid shapes which could be logs or crocodiles. He told himself that the scene had the sad, lovely serenity of an old Chinese painting: a stylized beauty which needed no human to give it its charm and one which he had loved before *that* terrible thing had happened to him. '*Beauty,*' he whispered to himself in his strange, hoarse voice, the product of plastic, metal and the art of a Red Army surgeon, as he stared down at his withered black talon of an arm. *Beauty*, when the only women who would accept him were the most hardened and patriotic cadre members, and when every time he entered a conference with Giap and Ho, there was a hurried, frightened intake of breath; when even his own fanatical Death Volunteers shivered at the sight of his terrible ruin of a face so that he had to keep it permanently hidden from them, behind the damned mask. What did such concepts mean to him? All he knew and cared for now was death, the final, long-awaited boon of oblivion. Captain Napalm looked at the green-glowing dial of his watch and then whispered to the commander of the mortar platoon standing next to him, 'Twenty-five more minutes, comrade.'

'Victory, Comrade Captain,' the bow-legged gunner whispered back in the routine greeting of the Viet Minh.

'Victory, Comrade,' Captain Napalm answered, but at

the back of his mind the hard little voice whispered another word, one which gave him more pleasure. It was simply *DEATH*.

There was little sound in the compound now, save the moans of the seriously wounded as Schirmer, accompanied by Schulze, did his rounds of those who were to stay behind and cover their departure. They paused at the hut which accommodated most of the seriously wounded, their faces ashen with shock, the purple-pencilled drug dosages marked on their sweat-damp brows. Schirmer looked at the still bloody bodies and then at Schulze. The big NCO shrugged. 'We can live in hope, sir,' he whispered, 'but for my money, the Slant-eyes'll probably croak the lot of them as soon as they've taken the camp.'

Schirmer sighed but said nothing. Some of the men lying packed together on the dirt floor had been with him eight long years. It hurt like hell to abandon them just like that, but there was no other way. Hadn't the motto of the Headhunters been all along '*March or croak*'? They couldn't march any longer.

Slowly he climbed down the rickety wooden ladder, followed by Schulze, to where Sergeant Daux squatted on the ground behind the machine-gun, a cleaning-rod acting as a tourniquet for his shattered right leg and a blood-stained bandage around his head. He tried to struggle to his feet when he saw the CO approach, but Schirmer waved him to remain seated among the circle of other wounded who were staying behind to man their weapons. Daux was still bleeding badly in spite of the tourniquet, and by the faint light, Schirmer could see he was sitting in a pool of his own blood.

Biting his bottom lip, Schirmer asked, 'Do you think you can make it, Daux?'

'Easy as pissing in me own boot, sir,' Daux answered, the old indomitable grin splitting his tough veteran's face. 'Worse things happen in a shitting kindergarten.'

Schirmer forced a grin. 'They'll come after the mortar barrage. If you could keep them off for' – he shrugged – 'perhaps five minutes, we'll . . .' His words trailed away a little hopelessly, knowing that he was leaving this old Head, who had been with the 666th SS Para Battalion before they had broken out of the Ivan POW Camp so long ago that Christmas*, to his death – or worse.

'Never fear, sir,' Daux said. 'Me and those hairy-assed mother-humpers,' he indicated the pathetic circle of wounded men, 'we'll probably be able to keep the Slopeheads off for the rest of the war. I've shate better soldiers than those Slant-eyes. Wet dreams – the lot o' 'em!'

'Good man, Daux,' Schirmer turned away, too moved to continue.

Daux winked at Schulze. 'Give one of them slits back in Saigon a poke for me when yer get back, Schulzi.'

'Get off it!' Schulze growled with forced roughness. 'You know you never liked girls anyway, Daux.' He touched his right eye in awkward embarrassment. 'Look after yersen, you old bastard.'

'Same to you, Schulzi.'

'Thanks.' Without another word, he turned and followed Schirmer to where the long, dark files of men were forming up to begin their silent progress down to the water, each second man carrying the log that would bear him and his team-mate down the river.

Noiselessly, boots covered in the spare pair of socks, each man, with his right hand on the shoulder of the man in front of him and guided by the whispered directions of the NCOs who were posted hidden in the bushes along the route made his way down to the dark-running river.

There a tense, anxious White Lightning, his grease-gun at the ready, waited for them, flashing his eyes at the opposite bank every couple of seconds to check whether the Slant-eyes had been alerted. But from that direction came no sound save the plaintive notes of the marsh birds and the hollow gurgle of water running from some side stream into the river itself.

The first teams began to place their logs on the water and clamber upon them, while White Lightning held his breath, telling himself that they seemed to be making enough noise to awake Uncle Ho himself in faraway

*See *Hellfire* for further details.

Hanoi. One after another, lying flat on the logs, the teams started to make their slow progress down the dark river, floating right beneath the noses of the Death Volunteers.

The minutes ticked away leadenly. Time and time again, an anxious Schirmer, his nerves jingling electrically, glanced at the green-glowing dial of his watch. It wouldn't be long now before the Volunteers launched their attack. He could already sense them massing in the bushes all around. Time was running out fast.

'All right, Skipper.' It was White Lightning. 'The last batch is off. It's our turn now.'

Schirmer flung a last glance back at the stark black outline of the stilted huts where the handful of seriously wounded prepared for their last battle against the Reds whom they had fought for so long in a dozen countries. Slowly he raised his right hand to the peak of his kepi in silent salute. Businesslike again, he whispered to Schulze, 'All right, swing aboard and watch you don't fall off, you big rogue.'

'I joined the shitting Army, not the Navy!' Schulze growled throatily and, grappling a little, clambered on to the next log, followed an instant later by Schirmer. He kicked out. The log left the muddy bank. Instantly it was seized by the current and carried into mid-stream, the two lone men on it rigid and fearful, trying to make the smallest possible target.

Faster and faster they started to run towards the narrow chasm, picked out by the flush of white water, which led out of the little delta in which the village nestled. Hardly daring to raise his head, Schirmer watched the rushing whiteness grow ever closer. Suddenly things started to go wrong. As log after log cleared the narrows, their own log was caught by some sort of undercurrent. To his horror, Schirmer realised that they were going to be borne to the bank held by the Volunteers. 'Goddam, Schulze,' he hissed fervently, 'paddle her off!'

The big NCO needed no urging. He saw the danger at once. His big hands flailed the water with all his strength. Schirmer did the same, hoping the noise of the water rushing through the chasm would drown the noise they were making. Furiously, sweating heavily, the two men paddled and paddled. To no avail! The log, completely

out of control, smashed into the rock side. In an instant it
had pitched them into the water. But even the shock of
that ice-cold douche could not overcome the one caused
by the sound of many bare feet shuffling through the
damp grass towards them, only metres away. Schirmer's
heart seemed to stop beating. They were trapped in the
midst of the Volunteers!

Phoosh! The flare hushed into the night sky.

'*Duck!*' Schirmer shrilled.

As one they buried their heads in the wet mud. The
flare exploded above them, bathing the scene below in an
eerie, glowing, icy-white light. Desperately, Schirmer
buried himself in the stinking mud and sought for the
trigger of his grease-gun, praying that the muzzle was not
full of dirt. The bastards wouldn't take him alive. They
were almost on top of them now. How could they possibly
not spot them!

An obscene howl. A spurt of scarlet flame split the
darkness and the first mortar bomb shot above their prostrate bodies. A thick crump, and the night was full of
hissing steel splinters.

'Christ on a crutch!' Schulze breathed with relief. 'Let's
get the shit out of here, sir. They – ' The crump of the
next mortar bomb drowned the rest of his words.

Propelled by a sudden charge of renewed energy,
Schirmer started to crawl through the mud of the bank,
while the barrage rose to a fearsome crescendo. His heart
beat like a triphammer while his eyes searched the glowing darkness for the first sign of a human figure which
would herald curtains.

Crump . . . crump . . . crump . . . The last three
bombs exploded. The loud echoing silence was broken
the next instant by the cheers and bugles of the Volunteers as they charged forward to the water's edge.
Schirmer felt a naked foot press him deeper into the
mud – then another. Carried away by the drugs and their
excitement the racing Vietnamese did not notice the two
men. They hit the water at full pelt at the same moment as
the machine-gun manned by the dying Sergeant Daux
chattered into action, sending glowing tracer hissing
across the river.

'Come on!' Schirmer hissed, rising to his feet. 'Let's

hoof it while we've got the chance.'

Blundering their way through the racing figures every-where, intent on getting across before the machine-gun swung back in their direction once more, the two Germans pelted for the cover of the jungle beyond where they knew that the rest of the Headhunters would be waiting for them in anxious expectation.

Five minutes later they had joined up with the rest and crouched there, dripping wet and broken-lunged, listen-ing horror-stricken, the small hairs at the back of their heads erect from dread, to the piteous screams and dying wails of the wounded men being massacred in the village beyond, until finally the last desperate pleas were drowned by the slow beat of the Slant-eyes' automatics and silence descended upon Massacre Valley once more.

NINE

Colonel Mercier sweated at his paper-littered desk in spite of the electric fan whirling round at full power and the glass of ice-cold Chablis which he sipped nervously every few minutes.

Outside it was Saigon's rush-hour. The broad street was filled with a kaleidoscope of an empire in decay: delicate young prostitutes in varicoloured *ao-dais*, wearing conical sunhats or soliciting from beneath their parasols; tough bronzed legionnaires and pale-faced, helpless recruits just in from Marseilles; legless veterans hobbling along on their crutches or begging at street corners that stank of cats' piss and rotting fish guts; suspicious looking characters from the country squirting streams of pink juice in the paths of the soldiers and revealing mouthfuls of black teeth when they did so; important, plump, pompous officials in their black limousines, their way being cleared through the mess of cycles and rickshaws by the screaming sirens of their motorbike outriders; and in front of every bar or store frequented by the colonials the sandbags and grenade-proof screening of a capital city under siege.

Mercier took another sip of his Chablis, wishing Lequen would hurry up. He flashed yet another look at the wrist-watch which adorned his one arm. His spy at High Command was late. He frowned. Everything seemed to be going wrong. It was now nearly a week since Schirmer and his Boche had vanished into the jungle. Navarre still clung to his defensive strategy although there were obvious signs that Uncle Ho was up to something. And now, according to Lequen's hurried report over the phone, the Americans were applying pressure on Paris in order to get things moving again in Indo-China. But the spy had been unable to say what the Americans wanted from Navarre: someone had just come into his office.

Mercier glowered at a couple of slim, hipless young

men in white shirts and severely tailored black trousers walking hand in hand, one of them white and obviously French. Corruption and perversion everywhere, he told himself. Wasn't it because of such things that he had been forced to find his Boche mercenaries to fight France's dirty war for her? '*Mon Dieu*,' he moaned aloud. Did France deserve to be saved?

'Sir.' It was Duclos, the little hunch-backed corporal who was his trusted servant and who looked so incongruous in the uniform of the Legion with his misshapen back and metal-rimmed spectacles.

'Lequen?'

'*Oui, mon Colonel*.'

Lequen looked like any other of the elegant staff officers at Navarre's HQ, whom Mercier privately described as puffs, pansies and pederasts, save for one thing – a black patch covered the spot where his right eye should have been. He had lost it in the winter offensive of '52, when he had been serving with the Legion before transferring back to the regular Army. The young lieutenant saluted in the slow casual manner of the High Command and grinned, 'What is your nationality, soldier?'

Mercier grinned back despite his worries and played the little private game. 'Legionary*, *mon Général*. Sit down, Lequen, and give me the dirt.'

Lequen's grin vanished as he sat down and waited for Mercier to commence.

'All right, let's have it, Lequen.'

'This morning, Colonel, it came. Those parlour pinks in Paris have yielded to American pressure. If they're going to pay for the war, they maintain, they want some say in its direction.'

Mercier nodded his understanding. In spite of the fact that he heartily disliked the Americans, he saw their point. 'And what do they want?'

'Action, Colonel.'

Mercier laughed. 'Not only are the Americans optimists, but they are fools, too. Action from General Henri Navarre – *impossible*!'

*A famous saying in the Legion based on an interchange between the celebrated General Lyautey and an unknown Legionary in the nineteenth century.

Lequen smiled at the red-faced colonel winningly. 'Ah, but there you are wrong, *mon Colonel*. Our beloved Commander-in-Chief is finally going to bestir himself. Monsieur Maginot, as some of us at HQ call him behind his back, has decided that your warnings of some sort of Viet Minh offensive before the monsoon season might have an element of truth in them, and he is preparing to act.'

'*What*!'

Lequen touched his eye-patch delicately, as if to reassure himself that it was still there, and said, 'Yes, indeed. He has decided that if the Viet Minh attack from the north, it will be through the Thai mountains into the Red River delta and on southwards.'

'And?'

Lequen's grin vanished. 'And he has decided to reinforce the fortified hedgehog at Dien Bien Phu to the tune of sixteen thousand men. As Navarre, our latterday Napoleon, sees it, the Americans will be satisfied he is doing something, and that will get those parlour pinks in Paris off his back; at the same time, he'll be continuing his old defensive strategy. According to what he told his staff intimates yesterday in the senior officers' mess, *if* – and he emphasized the "if" – Uncle Ho's boys attack, Dien Bien Phu will be turned into a battalion meat-grinder for them. The Viets will bite their teeth out upon it.'

Mercier slammed his one fist down on the table so that the ink-pot rattled. 'The fool – the blind, cretinuous fool!' he roared, crimson with rage. 'God in heaven! That damned Maginot Line mentality will be the ruin of France.'

He rose to his feet and stomped up and down the office in his gleaming, spurred riding boots, while Lequen watched him in anxious silence. Suddenly the little colonel stopped and gestured at the big map of Indo-China which decorated one wall. 'Look at it! Look at that shitty fortified hedgehog of his at Dien Bien Phu! A hundred square kilometres of valley surrounded by enemy-held jungle and mountains, which will depend upon its air strips for supply and reinforcements. At the best, Uncle Ho could mask it by a mere regiment and then continue southwards, leaving the garrison to sit on their fat arses and play cards. It would be May, 1940, in France all over again.'

Miserably Lequen nodded his agreement.

'And at the worst, Uncle Ho could make an all-out attack on the place – begin a siege – and France might well have a second Stalingrad on its hands with sixteen thousand French soldiers going into the bag. What a tremendous propaganda victory that would be for Uncle Ho!' He glared at Lequen as if he were the Viet Minh leader personally.

Lequen seized his opportunity to speak. 'I agree with all your points, sir,' he said carefully, 'but you are forgetting one thing.'

'And that is?'

'The air strips at Dien Bien Phu. As long as they continue operating, the place can hold out against the Slant-eyes.'

'Yes, the air-strips.' Mercier's rage at Navarre's defensive mentality vanished, as he considered that possibility. 'Hmmn, you're right there, Lequen.' He puffed out his red cheeks in Gallic exasperation. 'If we only knew what was going on in the damned Massacre Valley, then I think we'd have the answer to the whole problem.'

'You've not heard from the Boche?'

Mercier shook his head and stared out of the window at a fat pudding-faced Vietnamese woman under a huge cartwheel straw hat, who looked as if she had come straight from the paddy-fields, selling contraceptives to hangdog, red-faced recruits just off the boat. 'You like my daughters,' he could hear her crooning in bastard French. 'Cherry girls – very cheap . . . Number-one jig-jig, you like . . .'

Corruption, corruption everywhere, from top to bottom, he told himself.

'Where do you think they are at this moment – roughly – sir?' Lequen broke the uneasy silence.

Mercier took his gaze from the window. 'I don't know, but I do know where I could find out.'

'Where, sir?'

Mercier did not answer his question at once. instead he asked one of his own. 'Lequen, how do you fancy taking a little jaunt this weekend instead of wasting your time fornicating with that rather flighty staff colonel's wife?'

Lequen flushed a little and Mercier laughed. 'My good Duclos has very good eyes, in spite of his glasses. Little escapes him.'

'Obviously, sir,' Lequen said. 'But you mentioned a little jaunt?'

'Yes, to Dien Bien Phu. That's our closest base to Massacre Valley. If and when Colonel Schirmer's Boche come out, it'll be the place they'll head for first – and I'd like to be the one who receives whatever information they bring with them first before it is conveniently lost by General Navarre's tame intelligence boys, if you understand what I mean?'

'I do, sir. But how do we get there? Number One priority for aircraft is for reinforcements. It might take us a week to get a seat.'

'You'll come along then?'

'Of course, sir. Anything to get out of that perfumed cage of an HQ for a while. Dien Bien Phu is not exactly the front, but it might remind me that I am still a combat soldier instead of a general's flunkey.'

'Good!' Mercier beamed at him and rang the bell on his desk.

Corporal Duclos sidled in at once, eyes gleaming behind the thick-lensed metal glasses, almost as if he had been listening behind the other side of the door. 'Sir?' he enquired.

'We want to fly to Dien Bien Phu this weekend. Can it be done, Corporal?'

'It depends upon the size of the dash,' Duclos answered, as if there was nothing extraordinary in the fact that French officers had to bribe another French officer to get a ride in a plane.

'Money or dope?' Mercier asked.

Duclos gave one of his sly, lop-sided grins. 'Colonel, now who wants the franc these days, except fools? *Dope*, sir, it is obvious.'

'I'll see it's taken care of. We get the ride?'

'You do, sir.'

Mercier beamed at him maliciously. 'Not *you*, my dear little cripple – *we*. We are all going to Dien Bien Phu. I might have need of your particular talents to get us out of the place smartly.'

'As you wish, sir,' Duclos said without a change of expression.

Mercier laughed, but there was no humour in it. 'So we go to the wars. Three cripples – one blind, one lacking an arm, and Duclos with his poor twisted back. Gentlemen,' he looked at Lequen and then at the little corporal, 'are we not the symbol of *la belle France* in this year of 1954?'

TEN

It was an afternoon of grey cloud. Although it was long before the monsoon season, the peaks of the dark-green, jungle-covered mountains were already hidden in a thick mist, and a strong wind drove chilling raindrops, that stabbed at the Headhunters' laboured, strained faces like a myriad stilettos, down the valley. To Schirmer, marching as usual at point with Schulze and White Lightning, there was something sinister and threatening about the great sweep of forest, hung with wisps of fleecy vapour. All the same he was glad of the cover that the rain afforded.

They had been marching north-west two days now, ever since they had escaped from the village, and he was confident that he had fooled the Death Volunteers as to their route. Fortunately for the Headhunters, the enemy had shot the handful of wounded holding the compound in the heat of battle before they had thought to interrogate them. That had given them a headstart.

Schirmer had taken care that the Headhunters commenced their escape by wading four kilometres down river so that they had left no obvious footprints before they had entered the jungle again. In spite of the fact that he knew he had thrown off the chase, Schirmer had an uneasy feeling that they were not alone in the rain-drenched jungle. Time and time again he caught himself throwing an anxious look to his flanks or rear, overwhelmed abruptly by the feeling that the passing column was being observed by hostile eyes. But always there was nothing there. Twice, however, they had heard faint calls carried to them by an abrupt gust of wind, and early that morning they had come across a rough bamboo and grass shelter of the kind erected by the Viet Minh sentries to protect themselves against the elements during the monsoon season.

Now, in spite of the weather, the point picked their way

warily, keeping an eye open for *punji* stakes and booby traps, each man with a small phosphorescent leaf stuck on his pack so that the silvery glow was visible to the Headhunter following him at twenty-five-metres' distance. At the hourly five-minute break the weary Headhunters would stagger off to the cover of the nearest bush to rest but also to watch the flanks in absolute, tense silence. Like their colonel, the troopers knew that the enemy was close – very close – now.

It was about five, with the rain streaming down in a solid grey wall and turning the ground into a thick red goo so that their boots were great clods of mud, as Schirmer was beginning to consider where they would make camp for the night, when a sudden burst of rain-soaked wind carried the sound in their direction. Schirmer halted the column at once, cocking his head urgently to one side. But already it had gone, the wind having changed direction yet again. He turned to a stony-faced White Lightning. 'Did my ears mistake me?' he asked the American.

The latter shook his head slowly, as bewildered by the sound as the tall colonel was. 'No, you heard it, Skipper, all right.'

'But picks and shovels – *in the jungle*?'

'Roger and out. Picks and shovels it was, Skipper!'

'But what the devil could they be doing out here?' Schirmer exclaimed.

'Well, there's only one way to find out, sir,' Schulze said after a moment, wiping a great dew-drop of rain off the end of his red nose with the back of his hand. 'Have a look-see.'

Schulze, carrying the little patrol's only silenced grease-gun, wrinkled up his nose, sniffed and whispered, 'Sweet potatoes, rice and curried fish. Christ, my guts are doing flip-flops as it is!'

Schirmer rubbed the rain from his face and stared thoughtfully at the grove of trees from behind which came the faint chatter of Vietnamese voices and the smell of pungent Slant-eyes' cooking.

The rain was pouring down with tropical fury, dripping in a never-ending stream from the trees, virtually drowning any sound the handful of Headhunters crouched in the cover of the bushes might make. Schirmer considered their position for a moment, grateful now for the rain. With the handful of men under his command, he might be blundering into something more than he could handle; all the same, he was sure that what lay beyond the trees would finally reveal the secret of Massacre Valley. In spite of the risk, he knew that he must go on.

'All right,' he ordered softly, 'we're going on. If we run into anything we can't dodge, use your knives and fists. Schulze, you'll fire the grease-gun only in the last resort. Clear?'

'Clear, sir,' came a chorus of whispers from the soaked, tense men of his patrol.

Schirmer drew a deep breath and tapped the top of his jungle boot to reassure himself that his combat knife was there. 'Follow me.'

Strung out in a single file, their shoulders bent against the hissing rain which bounced off their bodies in little white spurts, the patrol moved into the trees, carefully skirting the spot beyond from which came the sing-song chatter of Vietnamese and the smell of cooking. They came to a small, eroded embankment, now a sea of mud. One by one they slithered down it, making an impossible noise, while the others covered the sliding man, their weapons at the ready and their hearts beating furiously. At the bottom Schirmer held up his hand for them to halt, his every nerve jingling.

There was the snap of a twig cracking. They froze. Had they been discovered? A small jungle deer came out of the trees, its ears pricked up and nostrils twitching. It stared at them with its delicate dark eyes yet seemed unable to make them out. Suddenly, with a high jump and a flash of white stumpy tail, it was off, crashing through the trees.

Schirmer swallowed hard. Behind him Schulze said in a weak voice. 'I beg to report, sir, I've just pissed mesen!'

Schirmer was too tense even to attempt a grin.

They pushed on, clambering over some wet, slippery rocks, and emerged from the trees into man-high ferns and undergrowth which still obscured their view of what lay ahead. Carefully, very carefully, aware now that the ferns might give way to open country at any moment, they crawled forward, with Schirmer in the lead. They parted the fronds in front of them, like curtains, not noticing the thorns which tore and scratched at their flesh cruelly as they did so. Schirmer pushed aside the last frond and thrilled with fear.

A skinny yellow face was staring at him, the dark eyes locked on to his in fear and shock. *What was this Round-eyes doing here?* The Slant-eyes hesitated and then opened his mouth to sound the alarm.

Schirmer was quicker. One hand shot out and smothered the cry, feeling the man's teeth bite deep into his palm, as his other hand fumbled frantically for the combat knife. Next instant, he had slid it smoothly deep into the little man's body between the third and fourth rib. The Slant-eyes body curved taut with unbearable pain. A moment later he was limp and dead in Schirmer's hands. Schirmer hung on to him like an exhausted lover, his eyes hardly able to comprehend what they saw beyond the murdered Vietnamese.

'*Great crap on the Christmas tree!*' Schulze breathed in awe, as they crouched there next to the body, staring at the sight in front of them. 'So that's what it's all about, sir!'

Schirmer nodded, not trusting himself to speak. Instead his eyes followed the four-metre-wide trail which had been hacked through the jungle, now a sea of mud but still definitely recognisable as the way along which the parked Molotova trucks, each one packed high with supplies and towing a 57mm field gun, would proceed once the track had dried out.

'They're recutting a shitting new road all the way from China down into the delta,' Schulze whispered, following the length of the track through the jungle until it disappeared into the rain-drenched gloom. 'And look at that camouflage!' He indicated the hundreds of trees on both sides of the track which had been drawn together by ropes and pulleys to form a leafy green arch. 'The Frog flyboys could fly over that for a month of Sundays and still not spot it.'

At last Schirmer found his voice, taking his eyes off the piles of tarpaulin-covered ammunition and supplies which were stacked on both sides of the track at regular fifty-metre intervals. 'You know what this is all about, don't you, Schulze?'

The big NCO, rain dripping from the peak of his soaked kepi, shook his head.

'Well, I'll tell you. Look at those trucks and those piles of ammo and supplies. They all add up to one thing – the Slant-eyes are going to use this track for a major surprise offensive into the delta. Perhaps the biggest offensive of the whole damned Indo-Chinese war! Why go to all this trouble otherwise?' He swallowed hard, as if he had just realised the full meaning of his own words. 'This is why they've tried to keep Massacre Valley under the wraps for so long.'

'And what are we going to do about it, sir?' Schulze asked in a small, awed voice. 'Have a go at trying to destroy it?'

'No, Schulze, for once the Headhunters are going to tip-toe quietly away, like the dog who after making love doesn't write.'

'But we'd have a helluva good chance under the cover of this downpour,' Schulze protested, but without too much energy in his broad Hamburg voice.

'Perhaps. But, Schulze, I think we'd better leave the decision-making about the – er – Red Highway to General Navarre and the perfumed gentlemen at High Command.' His mind made up, he rose and indicated the others should do the same. 'Come on, let's get the hell out of here before the rain lets up.'

One minute later the pouring rain had swallowed them up. The Red Highway was left to the parked trucks and the dead Vietnamese sprawled in the mud, as if he were sleeping . . .

ELEVEN

General Giap stared down at the crumpled body in the light of the hissing petroleum lantern, the rain dripping sadly from the brim of his solar topee. Next to him, Captain Napalm nodded to one of his Volunteers. The man parted the bushes beyond the body and flashed his torch. The marks of booted feet were clearly visible in the red mud. 'French,' General Giap said, almost as if he were speaking to himself.

Captain Napalm said nothing, the black mask limp and damp, sticking to his ruined face.

Giap considered. The coolie had obviously been murdered by the French force which Napalm's Volunteers had failed to liquidate, and it was obvious that the French had tumbled immediately to the purpose of the Red Highway. Bold as the enemy clearly were, they would have attempted to sabotage the track otherwise. No, they were on their way back to report their discovery; if they succeeded, it would not be long before the bombers came. Then his dream of the great battle which would shatter French power in Indo-China once and for all would be over. Uncle Ho would replace him, and there were plenty among the ranks of the Red Army who envied him and would be only too eager to take over his post. No, the French invaders must be stopped before they reached their own people.

Napalm, shrouded behind the silk mass and seemingly reading Giap's mind, broke his sombre silence for the first time since the discovery. 'Do not worry about their Air, Comrade General,' he hissed in his strange, distorted voice, which sounded as if it came up a series of metal tubes. 'In this weather, they will be impossible for the helicopters to pick them up.'

'The forecast?'

'It will continue like this for a further two days, Comrade General.'

'Good.' Giap's voice sounded a little more cheerful. 'Then you will have two days to find them, Comrade Captain.'

Napalm nodded and said nothing. Giap shivered a little as he looked at the sombre gaunt figure standing there in the dripping rain, whatever emotion he felt hidden by the mask. For the first time he realised just how very frightening Napalm was. He pulled himself together and wiped the raindrops off his broad, gleaming yellow face. 'What will they do, Captain?' he asked sharply, trying to overcome his silly moment of weakness by his brisk military manner.

'They are good soldiers, Comrade General, I know that now. They will enter the jungle again, avoiding our posts, and try to work their way through the Thai Mountains. Somewhere to the south of them they will emerge onto Route 41 beyond the Black River. There they will hope to be picked up by their Air. If the weather continues to remain bad and prevent flying, then they will attempt to make contact with French patrols from Dien Bien Phu.'

'Dien Bien – ' General Giap caught himself just in time. Even this fearsome, fanatical patriot standing opposite him in the dripping rain, who was dedicated to death for the cause, must not be told that great secret. 'But the jungle is large, Comrade Captain, and under these conditions your men will have difficulty finding them.'

'Not so.' He indicated the footprints in the mud. 'They will leave a trail, and even if they don't, this time we will not lose them.' Almost as if in response to a signal, there came the monstrous baying of dogs from beind Giap. Feeling the small hairs at the back of his head stand erect at that eerie sound, the general swung round.

Volunteers, barefoot in the ankle-deep mud, had appeared, their skinny arm muscles bulging as they tried to restrain their charges: evil black hounds, their little red eyes glowing in the hissing light of the petroleum lanterns and their huge dripping jaws open to reveal cruel yellow teeth.

'Thai hunting hounds,' Napalm hissed silibantly, his eyes glinting murderously from the twin slits in the silk mask. 'This time they will not escape me.'

Giap caught his breath. There was something frighteningly weird about the whole scene: the dripping rain, the gaunt masked man with his crippled arm, the evil black hounds. Angrily he told himself that for a great captain he had too much imagination; it was fatal for one who hoped to win a great victory soon. 'Good, Comrade Captain. Then you must set off at once.'

'My patrols have already begun to move out, Comrade General. We will now take over the point with the hounds.'

Giap gave him a fake smile of confidence and uttered the usual formula. 'Victory, Comrade Captain.'

'Victory, Comrade General,' Napalm echoed hollowly. Next instant he vanished into the jungle with his men, the black hounds already beginning to bay, as if they could scent their prey.

General Giap shivered yet once again and thanked the gods he no longer worshipped that he was not out there in the dark jungle to be sought out by such monsters.

The great hunt had commenced . . .

Two: The Hunt

ONE

'Our defence plan,' the smart young captain, who was acting as Mercier's guide explained as they stood there in the drizzle, their raincoats slick and shining, 'is based on a system of strongly-fortified posts, sited so as to be able to give each other supporting fire and established in a ring around the main air strip and the command post over there at Huguette.' He pointed his swagger stick at the low earth-covered outline of the fort to their right.

'Gabrielle is held by the 5th Algerian *Tirailleurs*, Anne-Marie by a Thai battalion, Isabelle by the 2nd Algerian *Tirailleurs* and a Moroccan *Goum*,' he continued, 'and so on. At Colonel de Castries's HQ we have the 2nd Legion and the Colonel's mobile striking force, the Legion's 1st Para Battalion.'

'Very pretty names,' Mercier sneered, 'but at least you have two battalions of the Legion here.'

The handsome young staff captain from the fort commander's staff did not seem to notice the sneer. 'All in all, we have sixteen thousand troops under command, most of them fighting men, plus a squadron of tanks and fifteen planes.' He pointed his stick at the landing strip where Morane fighters and B26s were parked, grey dripping outlines in the rain. 'We can take care of ourselves, Colonel,' he declared confidently, 'and *more*.'

Mercier halted and took in the scene. Dien Bien Phu, he knew, was very important strategically. It was only fifteen kilometres from the Laotian border and it was the junction of three main routes, one of them coming down from China in the north. But the ten-by-fifteen-kilometre

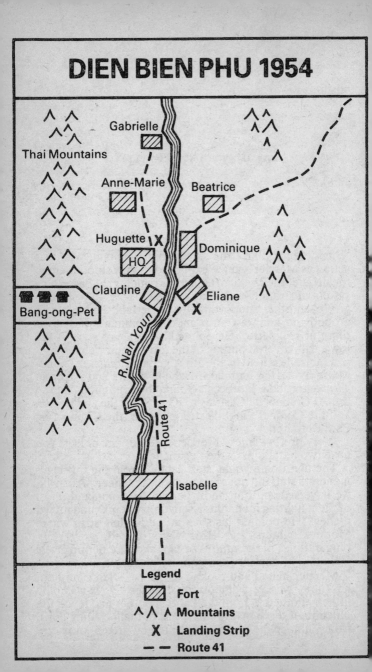

position was in a valley and it was dominated on all sides by a circle of heavily wooded hills roughly thirty kilometres in circumference. Strategically it might be very important but tactically it was far from ideal as a fortress; instead of dominating the surrounding countryside, *it* was dominated from all points of the compass.

'I don't know whether you did any military history at Saint Cyr, young man,' Mercier snapped maliciously at their guide, 'but perhaps you may recollect what General Ducrot said to Doctor Sarazin at the siege of Sedan in 1870?'

'I'm afraid I can't recall at this moment,' the young captain said a little helplessly so that Lieutenant Lequen standing next to him felt sorry for the guide.

'Well, I shall fill that particular gap in your education,' Mercier said grimly. 'The General, who was something of a rough diamond, took one look at his position and said to Sarazin, "Doctor, we're in a piss-pot and now the enemy is going to shit on us!"'

The captain flushed scarlet. 'I . . . I . . . ' he stuttered.

Mercier ignored him. Instead he said to Lequen, 'We're three hundred kilometres away from the nearest French garrison. Any attempt to relieve this place by land would be by tracks and roads ideally suited to ambush. Why, small, well-armed groups of Slant-eyes out there could keep whole armies at bay indefinitely.'

'Agreed, sir. But as I have mentioned before, there are the two landing strips. As long as they can function, the Air Force could bring in reinforcements and supplies.'

'On rainy days like this?' Mercier objected. 'Look, they are grounded at this very moment.'

'Yessir,' Lequen agreed patiently. 'But this is exceptional weather – it won't last more than a couple of days and the garrison has supplies enough for weeks. When the monsoon season starts, admittedly they won't be able to fly, but there again Uncle Ho's boys won't be able to attack either.'

'I suppose you're right,' Mercier said with some irritation. 'But woe betide us if the Slant-eyes ever manage to bring up heavy artillery. That landing strip will be a death-trap for the flyboys.'

Their guide laughed confidently. 'I doubt that, sir,' he

said. 'Uncle Ho and General Giap might be regarded in some quarters as rather clever, but even they are not *that* clever. The jungle out there is virtually impenetrable.' He smiled winningly at Colonel Mercier. 'They'll be lucky to get a handful of bods through it, not to speak of heavy artillery.'

'Let us hope you're right, Captain,' Mercier said without conviction. 'Now then, do you think we'll be able to see Colonel de Castries now?'

Colonel de Castries, tall, lean and a typical ex-cavalryman, rose as Mercier entered his office and extended his hand. 'Not another member of the Legion?' he exclaimed in mock wonder. '*Mon Dieu*, I think I'd better retire and leave the fort to you of the Legion – there are enough of you here at the moment.'

Mercier bit back his reply and forced a smile. 'Just passing through, de Castries,' he said, taking a seat while Lequen stood by the door. 'Wanted to pay my respects, ask a question and make a request.'

De Castries tut-tutted and signalled to the attentive orderly to pour them a glass of his favourite *eau de vie*. 'Why in such a hurry, my dear Mercier? We have a stream of visitors here – why we even had an American general the other day – but we rarely have visitors from the High Command. Stay and regale me with HQ gossip. Tell me about my first star, for instance.' A smile played about his long aristocratic face but his eyes were serious enough.

Mercier groaned to himself. Another one, a little voice within himself sighed. Out for promotion, regardless of what might happen to his men – or to France. 'A star, de Castries? Keep your nose clean here and ensure that Navarre gets his fifth, and you'll have it, my dear fellow.'

De Castries laughed easily and raised his glass in toast. '*A la votre!*'

'*A la votre!*' Mercier downed his fiery brandy.

'Here my nose remains as pure as driven snow,' de Castries said, signalling to the orderly once again. 'Nothing ever happens here,' he sighed and reached for his glass, 'and I doubt if anything ever will. We are simply just too strong for Uncle Ho and he knows it.'

'Hopefully,' Mercier said, almost to himself. 'Now, de Castries, have you heard anything of my Boche?'

'Oh, *those* chaps.' De Castries wrinkled his formidable aristocratic nose, as if in disdain. 'Nary a thing, I'm afraid. But then I've never worried much about the Boche, you know, Mercier.' He gave Mercier a fake smile.

'You should,' Mercier snapped, 'considering a quarter of your garrison here is made up of Germans serving with the Legion.'

'You said you had a request, Colonel?' de Castries said, stiffening visibly.

Mercier was not put off. 'Yes, de Castries. I want to have a look-see up that road to the north, Route 41 – and I'll need a platoon of infantry. In this weather it is impossible to fly, I should imagine.'

'Men? Out of the question, Colonel; completely out of the question. I need every man I've got here.'

'I thought you just said you were so strong?'

The ex-cavalry officer did not seem to hear. 'The hourly patrols we send out account for a large number of bodies. Manpower is a real problem.'

Mercier rose to his feet and touched his one hand to his rakishly tilted *kepi*. 'May I wish you all the best, de Castries,' he said easily.

'You are going?' de Castries exclaimed, surprised.

'Yes, I think I'll go and talk to the Legion,' Mercier answered and left, leaving de Castries to consider whether the one-armed colonel had really been serious about that star.

One hour later, Duclos's case of black market Scotch whisky had changed hands and the sick-bay of the 1st Legion Para Battalion had been cleared. A small packet of marihuana had been furtively passed on to the pale-face, sick-looking Algerian in charge of the motor pool, and two jeeps, filled up with gas, had been parked outside the sick bay, their motors running but their drivers vanished.

Two hours later, the small convoy set out, heading north: two jeeps and a half-track filled with eager but variously sick paras of the 1st Para Battalion, excited at the chance of action at last after four months of boring garrison duty. As Mercier commented to a grinning, one-eyed Lequen, who had still not overcome his admiring amazement at the way the hunchback Duclos had managed to provide the platoon behind de Castries' back, 'Its a case of the blind leading the blind, what, Lequen? . . . Now then, let's see if we can find out what kind of unholy mess those tame Boche of mine have gotten themselves into . . .'

TWO

'It looks too good to be true, Skipper,' White Lightning said slowly, lowering his binoculars.

Schirmer, crouched next to him in the dripping jungle, did the same, his face thoughtful. For nearly three days now they had been on the run, and for the last twenty-four hours they had been attempting to cross the Red River, which barred their progress into the delta to its south. But each time they had found a ford it had been guarded, and Schirmer had not dared to attempt a crossing in case the guards called up reinforcements. Now down there, only four hundred metres away, there was a perfect plank bridge – with not a guard in sight!

White Lightning rolled over onto his back in the wet fronds and looked up at Schirmer's lean, taut face. 'Nice and inviting, isn't it, Skipper? The only thing missing is a big billboard like we used to put up in the old 101st during the war – "Please cross, courtesy Uncle Ho and his boys."'

'Yes,' Schirmer agreed. 'You're quite right, Major. Somewhere over there they're wating for us to arrive and attempt a crossing.'

'Jesus,' the bald American breathed, 'they must be naïve to expect us to fall for that one! Even a bunch of rookies would know they were walking straight into a trap.' He stared at Schirmer's face and worn eyes, with the deep circles underneath them, revealing only too well the strain he and the rest of the Headhunters had been subjected to these last few days. 'You're not listening, Skipper?'

Schirmer shook his head. 'Oh yes I am, Major.' He looked directly at the American. 'You said trap. Perhaps we should do them the favour?'

'What?'

'Why not? The Slant-eyes have always believed that

they were the experts at jungle warfare – after all, the Frogs have made some terrible blunders in that field. Put ourselves in their place. Presumably they're thinking we're at the end of our tether now and we'll be ready to clutch at straws. That bridge, the way they see it, must appear like a godsend to us. A chance to get out of this damned jungle and head for base.'

'I agree with every word you say, Skipper. But it is still a trap, all the same.'

'Only if we don't know it is a trap, *but we do*,' Schirmer persisted, his mind racing as he started to work out his plan. 'Let me ask you a question.'

'Shoot.'

'If you were a conventional infantry officer, when and how would you cross the bridge?'

White Lightning answered at once. 'The texbook solution would be under cover of darkness, with scouts out checking for mines, booby-traps and the like in advance of the main force.'

'Exactly.'

'Now why shouldn't the Headhunters cross according to the book, eh?' Schirmer continued.

'Okay, I'll play the question-and-answer game with you, Skipper,' White Lightning said, puzzled. 'Because the Headhunters are not a conventional infantry outfit. We don't do things by the book like the Legs. That's why we're alive at this moment in spite of all the shit the Slanty-eyes have been slinging at us the last week or so.'

Schirmer forced a smile. 'Don't think I'm tormenting you, Major. In fact I'm just testing out my theories on you. You see, the men have had about enough. I've got to get them out – and soon. Not only that, we've got vital information for Colonel Mercier. That secret road spells trouble, and the sooner Mercier informs the brass about it, the better. No, Major, that bridge is our last chance and we're going to take it.'

'But it'll be sheer suicide, Skipper!' White Lightning protested hotly.

'Not if we do it like this. We make the conventional text-book crossing that the Slant-eyes will expect us to make, but by that time we've already got another force across and it'll be the Slant-eyes who will walk into a trap, not us.'

'But how are you going to get the first group across, Skipper? The river's not fordable at that spot down there. If it were, the Slant-eyes wouldn't have built a bridge.'

'I agree. But there are two ways to cross a bridge you know – above, *and* beneath . . .' And with that enigmatic statement, Colonel Schirmer rose from his hiding place, indicating that a puzzled White Lightning should follow him, and returned to where the Headhunters were resting in the cover of the trees.

The moon appeared from behind the drifting clouds and tinged the river below a faint silver. On the other bank there was silence, save for the croak of the frogs and the clicking sound made by a gecko lizard.

Schulze looked at his little party, all volunteers, each man with his face blackened, stripped of his equipment and armed solely with a silenced grease-gun and a combat knife. 'All right, you volunteers,' he whispered, 'we're off. And if any one of you makes as much noise as a sly fart, I'll have the eggs off'n him with a blunt razor-blade. Let's go!'

He reached up and, grabbing the wooden beam that supported the bridge above, raised himself effortlessly. Straddling the tie-beam above, he started to edge himself cautiously forward into the unknown. Behind him on the muddy bank man after man did the same.

Now the only sound was the soft ripple of the water below and the controlled, harsh gasps of the Headhunters made as they moved from beam to beam, each man knowing that any suspicious noise would bring the startling flash of light, the challenge and the swift metallic chatter of a machine-gun that would signal the end. In the lead, Schulze, in spite of an almost insane desire to get to the other side as swiftly as possible, took his time, pausing and cocking his head to one side to listen each time before he reached forward again to take a new handhold. Sound, he knew, carried a long way over water and he didn't want to have his eggs at the receiving end of any Slant-eyes' slug; not in that position anyway.

Once again, Schulze reached up and seized the next beam. Suddenly he gasped with horror. Something cold, damp, *and alive* touched his outstretched fingers. He froze, desperately fighting the almost overwhelming urge to whip back his hand. Behind him the long line of volunteers came to a halt, suspended now directly over the middle of the river.

Schulze drew a deep breath, trying to fight the harsh, choking gasps that issued from his parched throat. He peered through the gloom, aware of that live thing on his fingers but as yet unable to see it. The moon slid from beneath the clouds for an instant. The big ex-docker choked with sheer horror. Curled on his outstretched finger was the most deadly jungle snake of all, the little, vicious, sandy-coloured bamboo snake! His heart almost stopped beating as he fought the instinctive reaction to snatch back his hand.

The moon vanished once more, leaving him hanging there, not seeing the snake but sensing it in graphic, horrifying detail. The seconds passed with leaden feet. Would the snake never move? Behind him, someone whispered, 'What's up, Sergeant-Major?'

Schulze dared not reply. One false move, he knew, and he would be hurtling down to the water twenty metres below, already a dying man. The sweat standing in great opaque pearls on his tortured face and dripping steadily into his wide, terror-stricken eyes, Schulze prayed as he had never prayed before. *Make it go away . . . Make it go away . . .*

A thrill of absolute fear shot down his back. The bamboo snake was moving! He could feel its damp, cold slither across his fingers. Schulze's heart stopped beating. He willed his fingers to turn into stone. One false move now and he would be a dead man. The snake was still moving. He bit his bottom lip to stifle a scream of fear. Hot, salty blood flooded his mouth. *The horror was crawling up his outstretched arm!*

Now he could hear the faint rustle as the snake slithered up and across the naked flesh of his forearm, his skin a mass of horrified goose-flesh. Up onto the cloth of the shirt! Schulze's eyes bulged from his head. The snake was only millimetres away from his sweat-drenched face now.

His nostrils were assailed by a faint odour of decay. He fought back the desire to scream hysterically as the loathsome thing touched the tip of his chin cautiously, curiously, seemingly seeking its way. It made its decision. Slowly, infinitely slowly, it began to slither across the cringing flesh of his face, filling his mouth and nose with that terrible smell of decay, its wriggling belly making a faint wet sound as it rose ever higher. He pressed his mouth tightly closed, not even daring to swallow the blood which swamped his mouth. It reached his nose. *Would it attempt to enter his nostrils?* Hysteria almost overcame him. He could stand no more. He would let go and drop to the blessed obscurity of the water far below. *That thing burying its way into his head* . . . He couldn't take any more. His sweat-drenched fingers began to uncurl. This was it. He would drop now.

With a sudden spurt of speed and one last, terrifying, damp wriggle, the bamboo snake vanished across the top of his drenched kepi and was gone into the darkness, leaving him hanging there a limp wreck, with hot urine trickling down his right trouser leg unheeded.

Schirmer looked at White Lightning's taut face, faintly visible in the weak, silver shimmer of the moon. 'What do you think?'

'Don't know, Skipper. If they haven't made it, we would have heard shooting.'

Schirmer breathed out hard. 'They should have given the signal ten minutes ago. What in three devils' name is Schulze up to?'

White Lightning shrugged and stared at the stark black shape of the bridge outlined against the lighter night sky. Nothing moved out there; nothing stirred. All was peaceful – too peaceful. 'Well, Skipper, you've got to make a decision soon. Give it another fifteen minutes and that damned moon,' he indicated the scudding black clouds, tinged silver at their edges, 'will be out in full force.'

'I know,' Schirmer said unhappily, sensing rather than seeing the enemy already dug in on the opposite bank. 'I know . . . all right,' he made his decision, 'I'll go in with the point.'

White Lightning opened his mouth to protest, but Schirmer silenced him before he could speak. 'It's my plan and it's only fitting that I take the first bellyful of lead in case it goes wrong. All right, give me ten minutes, then bring up the rest.'

In a rare burst of emotion, White Lightning held out his hand to his CO 'Schirmer, you might be a Kraut and a bastard to boot, but look after yourself, *Kraut bastard*!'

Schirmer took the hand and gripped it hard, grinning in spite of his inner tension. 'I will, you hairless American arsehole. All right, let's get this show on the road now.'

Thereafter things happened fast. Some twenty men from Pansy Petersen's company slid out of the shadows, imitating the clicking sound of the gecko lizard to signal to each other, and began their slow progress towards the waiting plank bridge. Crossing the spongy earth at the river's edge, they were almost noiseless, but Schirmer in the lead, his grease-gun held in sweat-damp hands, felt very naked and vulnerable.

He stepped on the first plank. It squeaked alarmingly under his weight. Schirmer stopped as if shot, his heart pounding furiously. Nothing! The night was silent as ever. He gave the gecko signal once more, his rubber-soled jungle boots seeming to make a terrible noise on the wooden planks.

Halfway across he paused. On either side of the bridge, his men slid into the shadows, obviously as wound-up and tense as he was himself. Schirmer twisted his head round and listened hard. For a moment he did not trust the evidence of his own keen hearing. Then there it was again – the subdued clink of metal against metal! Across the water in the thick groves of trees that ran down almost to the river, someone was moving forward stealthily. Schirmer knew that they were waiting for the Headhunters now. Should he go on? There was perhaps still time to make a run for it. If only he knew that Schulze and his men were in position.

Schirmer bit his lip. With an effort, he took another step forward. The plank squeaked frighteningly. Behind him his men came out of the shadows. Slowly Schirmer moved forward, feeling like a doomed man being led towards the firing squad. In another few seconds he'd be at the other side. It must happen before then. *It must*!

The very stillness seemed unnatural – eerie. Schirmer felt cold drops of sweat trickle unpleasantly down the small of his back. Instinctively he tightened his grip on his grease-gun. Only ten more metres and he'd be across. His eyes tried to penetrate the silver gloom. Perhaps he had been mistaken. There had been no metallic clink. The other bank was not defended after all. By sheer naked willpower, he forced himself to take another step forward. Again the damned plank squeaked and made his heart leap clear into his throat.

Whoosh! The flare sailed into the air with frightening, electrifying suddenness. *Plop*! It exploded directly above the men on the plank bridge. They halted abruptly, their upturned faces bathed an uncanny, glowing blood-red. For what seemed an age, nothing happened. The men outlined high above the water appeared frozen thus for eternity. Then someone screamed in Vietnamese. A machine-gun started to chatter like an angry wood pecker. Behind Schirmer a Headhunter screamed, flung up his arms, his fingers fanning the air frantically, and slapped down face-forward on the planks.

'*Hit the dirt*, you – '

Schirmer's command was drowned by the tremendous blast of fire which hit the Vietnamese from the rear, as Schulze's squad went to work with their grease-guns. The surprised rebels didn't have a chance. Running down their line, dripping wet from the water in which he and the rest had been hiding up to their necks till this moment, Schulze fired short, sharp bursts into the lying men's backs. The night was hideous with their screams, yells, cries and shouts echoed back and forth between the wooded hills.

A group of Vietnamese broke ranks and sprang into the water. White Lightning's men, dug in on the opposite bank, opened up. The Vietnamese ran into a solid wall of fire. They melted away in seconds, their blood staining the tormented water red.

The guards on the far end of the bridge sprinted forward, running straight for a prostrate Schirmer. He didn't hesitate. His grease-gun chattered. The men went spinning to the left to slap against the beams, dead before they hit the planks.

In a matter of minutes it was all over and they were across, the chatter of the machine-guns giving way to the sharp, dry cracks of pistols as the Headhunters' officers strode through the dead and dying Vietnamese, applying their revolvers to the wounded's skulls and shattering them into myriad pieces with one swift bullet. The Headhunters were on the other side of the Red River.

THREE

They hit the village at the run. Grease-guns blazing, they ran from hut to hut, mowing down anyone in their way. Here and there the survivors from the river who had fled to the village tried to fight back, but they hadn't a chance. They were ripped out of their holes or from behind rocks, arms and legs torn to shreds by the terrific concentration of fire.

Incendiary grenades started to hiss through the air. The first bamboo hut went up in flames, the dry wood burning fiercely. Another followed, illuminating the panic-stricken women and children who ran back and forth, trying to find some escape, their numbers getting fewer by the second as the machine-guns tore them apart, heaping their bodies in screaming, twitching bloody pyres over which they threw gas and set it alight.

Schirmer dodged back as the gas exploded in a great, blue-red, searing blaze of light. At the far end of the village clearly visible now, there was a long line of barefoot coolies, pushing ancient cycles laden with a great pile of equipment. 'Stop those men,' he bellowed. 'Stop them – and get me a prisoner!'

'At the double!' Schulze yelled, kicking the Head-hunter nearest to him squarely in the seat of his pants. 'Come on, move, you slackarsed shit, you!'

The squad ran forward, firing from the hip as they did so, leaping over the twitching, writhing bodies of dying women and children. Schirmer followed, grease-gun at the ready. The coolies, taken completely by surprise – they obviously hadn't expected this kind of welcome in the remote village – dropped their bikes and turned to flee. Schulze's silenced grease-gun chattered noiselessly in his big hands. The first two barefoot coolies skidded to a sudden stop and dropped, their big straw hats oozing blood from a dozen holes. Behind them the others dropped to the ground, quaking fearfully.

Schirmer kicked the naked back-side of one of his men who had a dying peasant woman on the floor, greedily throwing up her skirts and fumbling with his flies at the same time. 'Pig!' he cried. 'Get up!' He ran on. Outside one of the huts an ancient, wrinkled, toothless grandma waved a skinny hand as if to greet him. At the very last second, he saw the stick grenade she clutched in her dirty claw. He fired a burst from the hip. She went down, blood oozing from her wrinkled, duglike breasts. Next moment the grenade exploded beneath her. She rose high in the air, her shattered limbs flying everywhere.

The firing was beginning to ebb away, to be replaced by the crackle of flames and the screams of the women as the Headhunters, working off the tensions and hatred of these last terrible days, started to loot and rape. Rifle butts cracked on unwilling skulls and women went down unconscious, to be taken next moment where they lay by crazy, screaming men. Knives ripped open tunics to reveal young, immature breasts. Teeth bit deep into nipples, while filthy, mud-crusted hands tore at flimsy underclothes. Fists smashed into bloody mouths over and over again until the gleaming gold teeth, set against a mess of red gore, were loose enough to be torn out. Slack-mouthed, wild-eyed men thrust themselves between the wide-spread legs of mere girls, while their gasping comrades, their chests heaving as if they had just run a great race, held their rifles poised at the heads of the screaming, hysterical victims.

But Schirmer had no eyes for the terrible scene. He had seen it often enough in the past; he would probably see it again in the future. It was part and parcel of the dirty war in Indo-China. He kicked a dying coolie in the jaw as the man tried to grab his foot. The man sank back without even a cry. Chest heaving painfully, he came to a halt in front of the little group of scared coolies, cowering next to the fallen cycles.

By the ruddy light of the burning huts, he could see the contents of the sack on the nearest cycle had spilled onto the ground. Curiously, he bent and picked up one of the slim, gleaming shells that lay there, while the coolies watched him with terror in their dark, slanting eyes.

'What is it, sir?' Schulze asked, watching him.

Schirmer did not answer at once. Instead his lips read the letters in the cyrillic script noiselessly. *M . . . O . . . S . . . K . . V . . . A . . . Moscow!* The shell was manufactured in Russia!

Schulze coughed, and Schirmer remembered he had been asked a question. 'It's a Russian 20mm shell,' he explained, 'meant for a quadruple flak cannon.'

'What?' Schulze exclaimed in surprise, his voice drowning the screams of the naked teenager who was trying to fight off the man who was trying to rape her and still hold on to his grease-gun.

'You heard, Schulze.'

'But . . . but what would those Slant-eyes want with a flak cannon out here in the middle of nowhere, sir?' Schulze asked in bewilderment.

'That's exactly the same question I've just asked myself, Schulze. Get the Schoolmaster.'

Tod, wiping the blood off his bruised knuckles but still savouring the beating he had inflicted on the girl before shooting her, arrived on the scene a few minutes later. Schirmer looked at him disdainfully and said, 'Schoolmaster, I want to know where these Slant-eyes are bound for – and quick.'

'Sir.' Tod launched a kick at the nearest coolie, smashing in his front teeth, and snapped something in Vietnamese.

The coolie, his eyes liquid with pain and terror, spat out of gory mess of teeth and blood and said something.

'What did he say?' Schirmer demanded urgently, as his men started to set light to the last of the huts.

'He's not a Viet, sir. I think he must be Chinese. I couldn't understand what he said,' the Schoolmaster answered.

'A Chink,' Schirmer said, puzzled. 'What the devil would the Slant-eyes be using Chinks as coolies for?'

'Perhaps they aren't just coolies, sir,' Schulze suggested, as the screaming survivors of the rebel village were forced to enter the burning huts. 'Just look at their feet. Plenty of blisters and corns. They've been used to wearing dice-beakers before someone transformed them into barefoot coolies.'

Schirmer followed the direction of his gaze and saw that

Schulze was right. Normally coolies had feet sheathed in such hard skin that they could walk over the sharpest rocks without injury; these men's feet were definitely not of that toughness. 'Chink soldiers?' he ventured.

'Could be right, sir,' Schulze said thoughtfully. 'They're sturdy enough and well-nourished.'

Schirmer looked along the line of prisoners. They certainly did look much better nourished than the usual sunken-chested coolie. But what in three devils' name were Chink coolies doing in the middle of nowhere, carrying flak ammo?

'Sir, if I might make a suggestion?' Tod broke into his puzzled reverie with his unctuous whine.

'Yes, do.'

'If they are Chinese and speak Cantonese and have got this far, they must have had someone to interpret for them, to obtain their rations, etc.'

'Yes, go on, Schoolmaster, pee or get off the pot,' Schirmer snapped, as usual unable to repress his dislike of the little ex-Gestapo sadist.

'Well, sir, let us find out who that man is – and treat him accordingly until he tells us what we want to know.' He looked down modestly at his long, cruel, splay-ended fingers. 'I don't think it would take me long to convince him to speak.'

Schirmer flashed another look at the prisoners, knowing as he did so that he didn't have much time to waste. The hunt for him and his men would soon commence again. 'They all look alike to me,' he exclaimed. 'I can't tell who is the shitting Viet among them.'

'We don't have to, sir,' the Schoolmaster said softly in that insidious manner of his.

'What do you mean?'

'Let me show you, sir.'

For the next five minutes the Schoolteacher worked quickly and efficiently, crooning to himself in a mixture of German and Vietnamese. He ordered each coolie to be stripped and spread-eagled between four short bamboo stakes driven into the soft earth, then wound a roll of fuse-wire about each man's body and finally attached a detonator to a small charge of plastic explosive slipped under his genitals. At first Schirmer was puzzled, then he realised what the little pervert was up to. The one man who would really understand what he was going to do would be the Vietnamese.

Finally Tod was ready. He took off his gold-rimmed glasses and wiped the sweat off them, blinking like a human owl. 'I think I'm ready now, sir.'

'Get on with it, man!'

Savouring his moment to the full, the Schoolmaster lit a cigarette with a flourish, staring down at the tied men. 'Now,' he said in Vietnamese, 'all I'd like from one of you is the answer to a little question. Just one and then you can go free.' He puffed out a stream of blue smoke. 'What are you doing here with flak ammunition?' His eyes beamed from behind the thick-lensed glasses.

No one answered.

'Tut-tut,' the Schoolmaster said mildly. He bent down and applied the glowing end of his cigarette to the fuse encircling the body of the man nearest him. It lit immediately. In a searing, white-hot rush, it ran the length of the man's naked stomach, while he twisted and turned frantically, screaming in agony as the tiny spurting flame burnt a bleeding, scorched path of red-raw flesh heading straight for his genitals. Just in time the Schoolmaster stamped his foot on it and clamped out the flame, leaving the man sobbing brokenly in Cantonese, with sweat pouring from his pain-racked body.

'Well, he's not our Viet,' the Schoolmaster said in an aside to Schirmer and then continued in Vietnamese, 'You see, my fine fellows, what is going to happen if I don't stop that fuse reaching your sexual organs.' He shrugged and snapped harshly. 'Now then, why are you here?'

Again there was no answer from the line of trussed-up prisoners, their dark eyes full of hate and fear.

'All right, have it your own way.' The Schoolmaster bent down and lit the fuse tied around the next man's naked body. Again it coursed fiercely across the stomach, ripping out the raw flesh agonizingly as the prisoner writhed frantically, his eyes bulging out of his terrified face as he watched the cruel flame race for his genitals. The Schoolmaster poised above him, smoking calmy, his foot raised ready to stamp the flame out. 'Just speak,' he whispered, his eyes sparkling behind the thick lenses. 'One word suffices.'

The tortured man, heaving at his bonds, gave out a strangled cry in Cantonese. The Schoolmaster's foot dropped. Next instant the little charge of *plastique* exploded. The man's spine arched like a taut bow. In his dying fury, just as the blood jetted up thickly and hot from the hole ripped in his loins, he burst his bonds. Next instant he slumped back dead.

'Swine,' the Schoolmaster said calmly, ignoring the sound of sobbing from one of the others, and wiped his blood-bespattered boot on the dead man's hair. 'Absolute filth.'

'Hurry, Schoolmaster,' Schirmer urged, sickened by what was going on here but knowing it was necessary. 'I think I can hear the sound of dogs.'

Schulze cocked his head to the right and heard the faint baying of hounds, too, 'You're right, sir. I've been hearing the shits off and on for three days now. They're on to us again.'

Hurriedly the Schoolmaster bent and applied the tip of his cigarette to the fuse-wire encircling a naked youth, a little skinnier than the rest of the prisoners and younger, with a narrow intelligent face. He raised his foot above it as it commenced its blistering race across the youth's tortured body as he writhed and heaved, nearly cutting his wrists through in his crazed efforts to break his bonds. 'Quick, boy, speak! Another five seconds and you'll lose your eggs. Speak now, damn you!'

'Stop . . . stop . . . F . . .' the boy screamed in Vietnamese and blacked out in the same instant that Tod's boot stamped out the flame.

'It's him!' he yelled in triumph to a sickened Schirmer.

'Bring him round – quick,' Schirmer ordered, as the howl of the dogs and the sound of many men crashing their way through the jungle got ever louder. Behind him White Lightning was already gathering the Headhunters together, kicking and pummelling them into some sort of formation, ripping them from the prostrate bodies of the naked screaming women. A Headhunter grabbed a bucket of slops from outside one of the fiercely burning huts and smashed its contents into the sweet-lathered face

of the unconscious youth. He came to, spluttering and
moaning, his eyes wild with pain and fear.

Tod towered above him, cigarette at the ready, full of
himself, enjoying to the full this moment of supreme
power; he savoured the look of fear in the youth's eyes
and his own gaze was riveted on the boy's genitals, hardly
able to contain his own desire. 'Well?' he asked in a
strangled voice.

'We have . . . come . . . down the Ho-Chi-Minh
Trail . . .' the boy groaned.

Tod translated hastily.

'The secret trail, I'll be bound,' Schirmer said. 'The
Red Highway, White Lightning,' he called, raising his
voice. 'We've got a lead. Go on, Schoolmaster,' he urged,
as White Lightning came running across while the
Headhunters began to take up their defensive positions,
ready for the attack that would come any minute now.

Tod thrust forward the burning cigarette, as if he were
about to light the fuse. The youth cringed and gabbled
something in Vietnamese.

'He says they are a detachment of the Chinese Red
Army, sir,' Tod translated.

'Bound for where?'

Schirmer did not need Tod's translation. He understood the name that came from the bound youth's
tortured, blood-stained lips. '*Dien Bien Phu.*' He flashed
White Lightning a significant look and rapped, 'But
why – why are they moving up there with flak
ammunition – '

The sudden howl of mortar drowned the rest of his
words, and suddenly all was confusion, with officers'
whistles shrilling, angry NCOs barking orders and the
Headhunters backing out of the burning village, firing as
they did so at the dark shapes of the Death Volunteers
and their great hounds as they came scurrying out of the
jungle, firing as they ran.

Schirmer cursed and then he, too, was running after the
others . . .

FOUR

'You will hang . . . the Fascist pigs,' the tortured youth gurgled, the blood trickling from the side of his mouth a deep black. 'Father Ho . . . must . . . avenge us . . .'

'Did they learn the truth?' Napalm whispered from behind his mask, staring down at the dying youth.

'No . . . we held out.' He flipped a weak hand at the line of dead Chinese. 'Avenge us . . .' His head dropped to one side abruptly; he was dead.

Captain Napalm stared down at the dead youth, ignoring the slugs still whining through the trees past the smoking ruins of the huts. Spurts of dust traced a path of dancing bullets at his feet, but he did not move, as if he were too deeply in thought to notice. At his side the young bugler flinched, but he dare not lose face in his commander's presence by diving for cover.

Around the two men, the village died. Most of the huts were now almost gutted. Bullet-scarred trees leaned down broken-limbed. Ash settled on broken and torn bodies. A naked baby pawed its dead mother's breast. A brown leg with a dirty, bare foot lay propped against a rock. Two dead children clasped in a permanent embrace, their skulls smashed in, were already attracting great greedy clouds of humming blue flies. An old crone of a woman in ripped bloody pyjamas crawled through the dust, drawing her intestines behind her.

Napalm did not notice. Like Schirmer, he had seen it all before. In his time he had participated in massacres, too. They were nothing new in the terrible war which had ravaged his homeland since 1940.

Suddenly his attention was caught by the group of his Volunteers, kicking and beating the terribly wounded soldier in the camouflaged uniform of the Foreign Legion who crawled before them, his hands making bloody imprints in the dirt. Napalm could guess what had happened. After capture they had shot him through both knee-caps. That way he couldn't escape, and if the Volunteers were forced to abandon him to the enemy, he would never be able to soldier again. Next to the gaunt, horrifying figure of the captain, the bugler jumped as one of the Volunteers crashed down the brass butt of his rifle on the prisoner's skull with a sickening crunch.

The prisoner, his face twisted and distorted with pain and with tears streaming down his cheeks, came to a stop in front of Napalm. The captain flashed a look of inquiry at the triumphant young lieutenant in charge. 'Legion, eh?'

'Yes, comrade.'

'French or German?'

The lieutenant shrugged. 'The pig doesn't understand French. I tried. Must be German.'

Napalm looked down at the man sprawled in front of him. In slow, careful but understandable German, he asked, 'What is the name of your unit?'

The grievously wounded prisoner looked up at him with a faint trace of his old pride. 'Special Para,' he croaked.

'And your commander?'

'Colonel Schirmer,' the man breathed, dying before Napalm's eyes.

'Schirmer. Note it well, boy,' Napalm ordered the bugler, without taking his hooded gaze off the German. 'Colonel Schirmer of the Legion's Special Para Battalion,' he whispered, almost as if talking to himself. 'He will pay . . . pay.' His voice rose. 'Lieutenant, attend to this pig.'

'Gladly, Comrade Captain.'

The Death Volunteer straddled the German as he crouched there, wrapping his legs around the thighs to give himself a hold. Then he drove his knife into the belly, ripping it upwards in a quick, brutal slash.

The prisoner screamed. His body rose from the ground, rigid, arched from the waist, his face contorted and his eyes bulging from his head. Next instant he fell back, dead. The Death Volunteer reached into the hole he had carved in the man's guts and ripped out the gall bladder. Grinning triumphantly, he held up the gory trophy for the cheering Volunteers to see.

'Enough,' Napalm snapped coldly, unmoved. Neither the manner of the prisoner's death nor his men's cries of triumph affected him. 'Get on with your tasks.'

The lieutenant tossed his grisly prize to the ground and, together with the rest, their smiles gone immediately, he padded off to the outskirts of the ruined village while Napalm considered what to do next.

He would not take his men into the jungle in pursuit as he had planned at first when he had heard of the local militia's failure to ambush the enemy at the bridge. Now he knew they were the most skilled troops in the foreign oppressors' army; they might well ambush him in the dense forest, and he did not want to sacrifice his life purposelessly in some obscure jungle skirmish.

Die he would. Die he must! With his ruined face, he could never live after the war was ended. But in the manner of his death, Napalm was selective. He wanted to die fighting in the great battle that General Giap had promised him would soon come. All the same, he wanted the men who had destroyed the village to pay for their crime – and to pay soon.

In his mind's eye he visualized the map of the delta. Before him stretching southwards towards the territory held by the French, there was the delta plain, covered by kilometre after kilometre of jungle. Knowing his enemy now, he guessed they would stick to it, although the going would be tough. Yet they had been on the run for a very long time now. Would they not be tempted to leave the jungle as soon as they were within marching distance of Route 41? Was their commander – this unknown Colonel Schirmer, whom, he had already promised himself, he would kill personally one day soon – strong-willed enough to keep them toiling their way through the impossible terrain a minute longer than necessary? Besides, couldn't he assume that Schirmer knew the secret of the Red Highway and would be all too anxious to pass on that knowledge to his own authorities? Napalm felt he would. But where would he try to join Route 41 . . . Where?

Suddenly it came to Captain Napalm. Behind the black mask, that horror which had once been a face cracked into a hideous parody of smile. He knew exactly where they would come out of the jungle, and when they did, he would be waiting for them.

'Bugler!' he rasped.

'Comrade Commander?' The boy took his eyes off the dead German with his guts ripped open, the flies already gorging themselves on the thickening black blood.

'Sound the advance!'

The boy raised his bugle to his lips and as the silver-clear notes rang out over the dead village, Captain Napalm could already visualize the Germans, at their head this unknown Colonel Schirmer, running straight into the massed machine-guns of the Death Volunteers. He shivered with sudden delight.

FIVE

The sun was rising higher. Now the morning mist was beginning to lift as the point hacked its way through thorny thickets that barred their progress, their machetes gleaming a bright red in the sun as they rose and fell rythmically.

All the previous day they had laboured in a distorted semi-circle across a spacious depression between a chain of forested hills, taking longer than Colonel Schirmer had estimated but avoiding the villages which he knew to be located in this no-man's land between the Viet Minh and French-held parts of Indo-China. As he knew from bitter experience, the villagers were pro-French when French troops were there in force and pro-rebel when the Viet Minh made their appearance in strength. Now when the Headhunters were not more than twenty-four hours from Route 41, Colonel Schirmer was taking as few chances as necessary – he avoided the villages.

As the cool mist began to disperse and the sun's rays intensified, the men at point started to sweat in the heat. Schirmer felt sorry for them as their shirts turned black with sweat while they hacked at the dense, bushy thorn trees with branches that reached almost to the ground joining the tangle of vines that lay there, but he knew he must concentrate on his compass. It was easy enough to begin walking in circles in the jungle where visibility was often limited to twenty metres. He concentrated on working out back-azimuths, trying to plot their course mentally without reference to the poor Japanese maps, made eight years before.

They were beginning now to work their way up into slightly more hilly country, where progress was hampered not only by the ubiquitous thorn brush and vines but also by piles of jumbled rocks. But Schirmer did not change course. He calculated there would be less likelihood of bumping into Viet villages in that kind of terrain.

It was about eleven when there was the first sign of trouble. They had just finished their hourly five-minute break and were beginning to struggle into their packs when it happened. There was the faint but audible crack of a single rifle shot. They went to ground immediately, their hearts pounding and their eyes straining towards the green wall of the jungle all around, their ears cocked for the snapping brush that would indicate the approach of the Slant-eyes. Nothing happened. There was no sound save the usual jungle noises.

'Check the column,' Schirmer snapped at Schulze, crouching next to him.

The word ran down the stalled line of sweating men. The answer negative. Nobody had been fired at and nobody had loosed an accidental shot. In the end a puzzled Schirmer gave the order to continue the march.

Thirty minutes later it happened once more. *Bang!* Again they flopped down in the long elephant grass, their hearts pounding and weapons at the ready, searching the trees for the first sign of the enemy. But none appeared. After a while, Schirmer looked at Schulze, no emotion in his eyes but his lean worn face grim. Schulze knew what his beloved CO was thinking. There was no doubt now. They were being followed; the shot was the lone pursuer's way of posting his comrades ahead of the Headhunters' progress. Schulze admitted it was a pretty fine way of getting on the column's nerves, and there was simply nothing they could do about it.

All that long afternoon the single shots followed them at regular intervals, as Schirmer worked his way ever closer to Route 41. After each hourly break the inevitable single crack of a rifle came in that same uncanny, unnerving way. About four, when the day sounds of the jungle were already beginning to fade away and the lizards' throaty screeches, which startled them still even though they had heard them a thousand times, grew fewer, Schirmer decided he could play the cat-and-mouse game, too. He hand-signalled a new course, moving the column more west than south. If the Slant-eyes were waiting for the darkness to carry out their ambush in the south, as he suspected they were, the longer it took the Headhunters to arrive at the spot, the more tense and jittery the ambushers would become.

Another half-hour passed. Further ahead, Schulze waved his hand. The point froze. Schulze hand-signalled a trail ahead. Forming a V with his sausage-fingers, he jabbed them at his eyes and then pointed north.

Schirmer repeated the signal but ended by pointing south. Schulze nodded his understanding. He moved away out of sight. Schirmer waited the agreed-upon ten minutes, allowing Schulze to check the trail to the south. Then he gave the signal to move forward again. Taking up the lead himself, he parted the brush and ferns which bordered the trail Schulze had spotted, double-tracked and well-used. For a moment he wondered whether it was linked with the secret highway they had spotted in the Thai Mountains; then he dismissed the thought and concentrated on the task on hand.

Schulze appeared round the bend, thumb raised in the signal of all clear. Schirmer nodded. The Headhunters started to move across in small groups, sticking to the hardpack so that the distinctive rubber cleats of their jungle boots wouldn't show up and reveal their numbers to anyone tracking them. Schirmer brought up the rear. Although he knew that the trail had been checked to north and south by a waiting Schulze, he still felt naked and vulnerable as he doubled across it to where the big NCO crouched in the bushes, grease-gun at the ready.

'What do you think, sir?' Schulze asked as they resumed their march westwards.

'They're waiting for us somewhere or other – that's for sure,' Schirmer said, his face set in a worried frown. 'They don't need a crystal ball to guess we're heading for Route 41.'

'When?' Schulze asked.

'As soon as it's dark,' Schirmer answered, staring up at the half-white of the sky above them which indicated that dusk would soon be upon them. He automatically noted that the single shot to their rear showed that their shadow was no closer. 'Come on, let's catch up with the others . . .'

With the light fading rapidly, Schirmer ordered out his sharpshooters, the battalion's best shots, each man armed with a telescopic, silenced rifle and his head covered by camouflaged netting. They took up the point now, well ahead of the rest of the column to which they were linked by a walkie-talkie. With a bit of luck, Schirmer reasoned, they'd see the ambushers before the Slant-eyes saw them. They would then set about their deadly work of cutting down Viet after Viet in the manner that the superstitious Slant-eyes dreaded. The unknown, unseen, unheard, sudden death. It was the Slant-eyes' own trick of using bow and arrows to demoralise French troops brought up to date.

Another party from Pansy Petersen's company fell behind. It was their task to plant booby traps for anyone following them on the trail. Swiftly they started planting the punji sticks they had been whittling for the last half-hour while on the march, dipping them in their own faeces and, for good measure, imbedding 'deballockers' in the ground: home-made bullet mines which exploded on contact from a foot, sending a 9mm slug hurtling for the unfortunate man's crotch. As Pansy Petersen chortled in his high-pitched falsetto to his sweating men, 'Won't we have a lovely lot of singing tenors this night, chaps, eh?'

In spite of his defensive measures, Schirmer was worried. The jungle and the darkness made it impossible or too dangerous to throw out scouts to his two flanks. Even if his counter-measures were effective to front and rear, dug-in Slant-eyes on both flanks might well massacre his long, straggling column. Then he recalled what they had done in the forests of the Ukraine when they had fought the Red guerillas at night.

It was tough on the men, especially in this murderous heat, but it would probably work. He ordered up the mortar section to the centre of the column and told the mortar sergeant to assemble his weapons on the march, commanding that instead of setting up the mortar base plate prior to going into action, the individual barrels would be held by the section's strongest men so that the column would have a form of mobile artillery ready to lob bombs onto each flank at a moment's notice. Thus the column straggled on, with the light almost gone and the nerves of each man tingling as they headed ever closer to the expected ambush.

Just behind a worried Schirmer, Schulze did something he had not done since he had been kicked out of his Hamburg elementary school at the age of twelve for having made 'a certain suggestion' to the needlework teacher (as the *Rektor* had phrased it delicately in the letter he had sent to Schulze's mother at the time) – he prayed, *hard*!

The night was warm, with hardly a breath of wind to cool the men's damp faces as they laboured up the long jungle slope where the trees had begun to thin out. Carefully the column kept to the far side of the crest so that they were not outlined against the background of the moonlit sky. Tired as they were from the long day's march, the Headhunters were tense and alert, knowing now that they couldn't be more than three or four kilometres from Route 41, which was patrolled regularly by their own troops. If the Slant-eyes *were* going to ambush them, it was more than likely that they were going to do it before they reached the road.

Schirmer, in the middle of the column where he would have the best control over the flanks as well as his front and rear, was in constant contact with the sharpshooters somewhere to their front, whispering continually into the walkie-talkie. For the last two hours there had been no single rifle shots to their rear and he reasoned that the man trailing them had already linked up with the ambushers, knowing that the Headhunters would change course no more.

Keeping clear of a large empty space in the trees, Schirmer waited for the clouds to obscure the moon for a while before ordering his men to skirt it, using the rocks for cover. Now no one was permitted to speak except himself and they kept contact by imitating the clicking sound of the gecko lizard and by hand signals. In case of danger to the rear and front, they were to imitate the call of the jungle owl, which flew at night.

The minutes passed leadenly. Schirmer could almost feel the tension in the air, and the sour smell of sweat which came from the men seemed to convey fear, too. He sensed that Schulze, as loyal as he was profane and tough, tried to keep as close as possible to him – and he knew why. If – *when* – they hit trouble, the big rogue wanted to be next to him, covering him with his grease-gun. Schirmer forced a smile. Schulze, like the rest of his Headhunters, was bearing up amazingly well, in spite of the tension and strain. There wasn't a finer unit in the whole world.

'*Erwin . . . hello, Erwin . . .*' The voice crackled abruptly in his ear-piece, startling him greatly although he had been expecting the call all along.

'*Erwin speaking . . . Erwin speaking . . . Problems?*'

There was a soft metallic chuckle at the other end. '*Not for us, Erwin, but for them.*'

'*Slant-eyes?*' he asked anxiously.

'*Ten of them, dug in to our right, about five hundred metres ahead of you, Erwin . . . Very sloppy bunch . . . We could smell that shitty rotten fish paste muck they eat a kilometre off . . . Orders?*'

Schirmer hesitated for only a fraction of a second before he snapped, '*Engage . . . Over and out . . .*'

In the very same instant that the walkie-talkie went dead at his ear, there was a faint jungle owl hoot to his rear. It was Pansy Petersen. They had run into trouble. *This was it!* There was no time to lose. Dropping all prohibitions about noise, Schirmer swung round and bellowed in the same moment that the first ragged snap-and-crackle of small arms fire to their rear indicated that Peterson had been attacked, '*MORTAR-MEN – LET'EM HAVE IT!*'

The biggest men in the mortar squad bent their backs, as the loaders dropped their bombs down the tubes which the big men bore and twisted the firing wheel. The tubes exploded, nearly throwing the living base-plates off their feet. With a howl the first mortar bombs began climbing into the sky, while the rest of the stalled column went to ground and peppered the jungle on both sides with screaming lines of tracer. They crashed down among the trees with scarlet, ugly flashes of flame illuminating the half-naked figures crouched there. Schirmer whistled softly. There were hundreds of them!

Further forward, the sharp-shooters went into action

with their silenced, high-velocity rifles. Within minutes twelve rebels were dead, drilled neatly through the head and falling onto the track with hardly a sound. Another group doubled forward to where the comrades lay sprawled like abandoned bundles of rags, puzzled obviously by the strange thing which had overtaken them but making no attempt whatsoever at concealment.

'*As ea-sy as pissing in yer boot!*' the NCO in charge of the sharp-shooters grunted as he nestled the stock of his rifle lovingly in his shoulder once again and took aim. He squeezed the trigger. The rifle jerked soundlessly. The rear man of the rebels' band threw up his hands in agony and went down as if pole-axed. The others ran on, unaware of his death. Now the sharp-shooters went to work with a will, ranging from rear to front of the running Slant-eyes. They exterminated a good dozen of them before the survivors became aware of what was happening and went to ground, trembling and fearful, not knowing what had happened – how their comrades had been struck down like this – and unable to find an enemy against whom they could fight.

The Headhunter sergeant grinned and whispered softly, 'Stop firing, lads, now. Let 'em cream their skivvies wondering how the other Slope-heads bought it.' He frowned at the increasing volume of firing to their rear and told himself that the main column was catching a packet. All the same, the way ahead was free. 'Don't worry,' he whispered, sensing the others' concern. 'We'll piss in Uncle Ho's beard yet!'

The mortar bombs had stopped the first fanatical charge from the left flank, but now the screaming Slant-eyes were coming in from both sides. The night air was full of the stink of cordite as the machine-guns chattered, swinging from right to left and mowing the Slant-eyes down by the score. Still they kept on coming, howling and screaming, firing wild as they came. *Snick . . . snick . . .* The brush all around, where the Headhunters crouched on the trail, was sliced by lead. Men yelped with pain and collapsed on the ground, to be dragged by the scruff of the neck to better cover by their comrades.

Schirmer, bent on one knee next to Schulze, firing controlled bursts into the still advancing Vietnamese hordes, felt the adrenalin pumping. His eyes seemed particularly keen and his mind worked with fantastic speed and tremendous clarity, all fear vanished now that he could see the enemy. He screamed involuntarily with the overwhelming elation of this great slaughter. 'Great buckets of boiling blood!'

Schulze chortled next to him, slamming home a fresh magazine into his grease-gun and ripping off another burst that tore the life out of a bunch of five Viets. 'This time we've got the Slant-eyes by the short and curlies. Lovely grub. Better than shooting yer wad – *almost*!' He fired another burst.

Now the Slant-eyes were only a dozen metres away. Taking tremendous casualties, the dead slithering back down the embankment, trailing blood behind them, and the wounded thrashing around in agony in the under-growth, they kept on coming all the same. '*Xung Phong*!' they screamed, the foam flecking their lips, their dark eyes wide and staring and crazy, '*Forward . . . forward . . . KILL!*'

Suddenly the moon vanished behind a scudding cloud. The Viets screamed in triumph. They increased the speed of their charge.

'Stand by with the bayonets!' Schirmer yelled in abrupt alarm. '*A la baionnette!*' He sprang to his feet and clubbed his grease-gun.

'Think this is a case for the Hamburg Equalizer,' Schulze said and hastily slipped on a great, gleaming pair of brass knuckles on his ham of a hand, just as the ter-rorists swamped their line.

In a flash all was murderous confusion. Now it was every man for himself. A bearded Slant-eyes rushed Schirmer, his curved sword upraised. Schirmer swung his clubbed grease-gun.

'Look out, sir!' Schulze yelled in alarm.

Schirmer hit the Viet a tremendous blow across the face. He flew through the air and slammed into the nearest tree, his neck broken.

Two Viets jumped Schulze. One springing on his back and wrapping an arm around the big Hamburger's neck tried to choke him. The big NCO roared like a bull. He lashed out. The cruel knuckle-duster smashed into the first Viet's sweating yellow face. The face burst like an overripe plum. The man went down, his features a mess of red gore. 'One down – ' Schulze bellowed in triumph, swinging round and trying to dislodge the man on his back, 'and one to go!'

The Viet hung on for all he was worth. His skinny arm dug ever deeper into the gasping NCO's throat. 'Apeshit!' Schulze cried in anger. Abruptly he ducked and heaved. The Viet flew over his head. Schulze sprang forward. His heavy boot stamped down on the other man's face, over and over again, as if he were trying to stamp out a fire.

Abruptly the moon came out from behind the black cloud. In an instant the trail was a glowing bright silver once again. The Viets recoiled. Behind them the second wave running out of the jungle hesitated, abruptly naked and vulnerable in the bright light.

The Headhunters reacted more quickly. 'On yer bellies – *fire!*' the NCOs screamed urgently.

The men needed no urging. Shaking off the last of the Viets who had broken into the column, they flung themselves into dust and loosed a tremendous volley into the surprised, stalled Slant-eyes.

Bits of bloody uniform and severed flesh flew everywhere under the impact of that terrible blast at such short range. The thwack of the bullets into the enemy's skinny bodies was clearly audible. They went down everywhere; screaming, crying, bleeding, falling. In an instant the flanks were littered with a heaving, blood-red carpet of tormented dying bodies.

Schirmer did not wait for them to recover. He sprang forward, grease-gun at his hip, crying, '*Forward – to the attack, comrades!*'

As one the Headhunters rushed on behind him.

The heart went out of the Slant-eyes' attack with dramatic suddenness. They broke. Fighting and clawing at those behind them and screaming with terror, they tried to escape the terrible vengeance of the white giants whom they had been so confident they would slaughter only minutes before, while behind them their wounded attempted to crawl and slither into the cover of the jungle only to be trampled down by the boots of the running Headhunters.

Five minutes later it was all over, with the Headhunters' execution squad moving from one wounded Slant-eyes to the next, literally shooting them to bits – first the fingers, then the nose and ears, finally the feet and kneecaps – so they would bleed to death, to be found later when their surviving comrades crawled out of the jungle: terrible warning of what happened to those who attempted to ambush the Headhunters.

Schirmer wiped the sweat from his dripping brow and turned to White Lightning, who was taking care not to look at the terrible scene and dipping the flesh wound on his hairless white forearm with his handkerchief. 'Squeamish?' he queried of the American, who after eight years still could not quite stomach the Headhunters' method.

White Lightning grunted something which Schirmer could not make out.

Schirmer shrugged and said, 'They made a shitting mess out of the ambush, didn't they?' curiously turning over one of the dead Viets with the toe of his boot to reveal a boy who couldn't have been more than fourteen. 'Poor little pisser,' he commented, looking down at those sightless eyes. 'Probably not even started five against one yet.'

White Lightning nodded. 'Very amateurish. Half-trained militia to my way of thinking – rushing us like that when the advantage was on their side. Sheer suicide!'

'Yes,' Schirmer said, abruptly weary, very weary. 'It was easy to take them – almost too easy.' He breathed out hard. 'All right, Schulze, get the men back in the column. Route 41 can't be far away now.'

'Did yer hear what the CO said?' Schulze bellowed above the firing of the execution squad. 'We're nearly home! Route 41's just up the trail! Those yellow slits in Saigon better start getting ready to open their pearly gates, 'cos Sergeant Schulze's on his way – and by the great God and all his triangles, *is he ready for it!*'

The tired laughter drowned the faint baying of the hounds up ahead . . .

SIX

It was a perfect dawn. The sky above the spiked-edged forest trees was calm and clear blue, indicating that it was going to be a very hot day. There was no sound save the chatter of the paddy-birds and the soft low of the plodding oxen, already being driven to the water-logged paddy fields by barefoot peasants, their faces hidden from the watching French soldiers clustered around the two jeeps and the half-track by their great, conical straw-hats.

Colonel Mercier breathed out a long stream of contented blue smoke and stubbed out the last of his *Gauloise*. 'Perfect, my dear Lequen,' he said and smiled at the younger man. 'One would think the dirty war was a million kilometres away.'

Lequen nodded and eyed the dusty bright-white of Route 41, stretching towards the mountains and running through the delicate green of the paddies which shimmered through the water. 'I heard firing during the night, Colonel . . . a long way off, but I definitely heard it, all right.'

'Could you locate the firing?' Mercier asked.

All that long week-end they had patrolled Route 41 with the sick legionnaires from the 1st Para, but they had discovered nothing. Schirmer's Headhunters had seemingly vanished from the face of the earth.

'I'm afraid not, Colonel.' He shrugged and swept his arm around to the north, past the peasants who were swarming into the paddies in surprisingly large numbers. 'Up there somewhere. If we only had a couple of choppers, we'd soon locate your tame Boche.'

'*If*,' Mercier laughed cynically. '*If* has been the operative word in Indo-China ever since I came out here in '45. *If* only we could get rid of the hidebound generals. *If* we could only have the entire Legion out here, instead of a bunch of pasty-faced, wet-arsed recruits. *If* we could only evacuate the whole of the male population from the whole of the north – *Merde, alors. If.*

Lequen laughed softly. 'You'll be advocating the final solution in a moment, Colonel,' he said jokingly. 'The concentration camps and the gas chambers, too.'

'Why not? Turn Indo-China into a country of women and children only and the rebellion is over. There is no Viet Minh.' He puffed out his rosy cheeks in the Gallic gesture. '*Fini la grande guerre!*'

'But public opinion back in France – '

'I shit on public opinion back in France!' Mercier interrupted him crudely. 'This out here in Indo-China is only part of a world-wide struggle, Lequen. While those pink pricks back there in Paris play games so that they can win the next shitting election, we're losing the war out here. Of course, that doesn't worry them. Indo-China is inhabited by niggers and Boche legionnaires only – who cares about them? But I tell you, my friend, when the Red Army's T-34 tanks start rolling down the *Champs-Elysées* then those white-gloved shits of deputies will really cream their striped pants.'

'Perhaps it has always been like that, Colonel?' Lequen suggested mildly.

'No, never. There have been other times when Frenchmen were proud of being French and were ready to fight their own wars; when they didn't need the Boche to do it for them; when they didn't collaborate with the enemy or sell him the machines and weapons with which he will beat us.' He thrust out his one hand in a gesture of exasperation. 'Oh, what does it matter?' He forced a taut smile. 'Forgive me, Lequen, for going on like that. I know your heart is in the right place. But it's this damned business with Colonel Schirmer's battalion. I am sure that he's found out what we want to know up there in the north and it's so damn frustrating not to be able to contact him.'

'I understand fully, Colonel Mercier. But you know I think our time is running out. General Navarre does expect his staff officers to turn up for duty occasionally.' Lequen indicated the soldiers slumped still half-asleep in the half-track. 'And we've got to get that bunch back to the First before Colonel de Castries starts making angry noises.'

'De Castries can go and piss in his boot,' Mercier began. He stopped suddenly, his attention caught by the hoarse baying of dogs far over on the other side of the paddy fields. He frowned, puzzled.

Lequen caught the look. 'What is it, sir?'

'Those dogs.'

'What about them, sir?' Lequen asked, following the direction of Colonel Mercier's gaze.

'What would Viet peasants be doing with hounds like that?' he indicated the tiny black shapes loping at the side of the far-away peasants leading the bullocks up the road beyond the ricefields. 'A dog like that takes a lot of food to feed.' He gave a short laugh. 'Hell, from what I know of the peasants, they'd rather roast an animal like that and eat it themselves as a treat rather than waste even household scraps on it.'

'Yes, you're right, sir,' Lequen agreed. 'One rarely sees a dog in their villages. Even cats are regarded as delicacies.'

Mercier made up his mind. 'Lequen, get those legionnaires on the stick.' He buckled on his pistol belt deftly despite his one hand. 'I think we'll go and have a little look at those happy peasants, eh . . .?'

SEVEN

In spite of the fight at the ambush and the night-long march, the Headhunters were making good progress, the trailblazers slashing away at the brush with a will and the two cartographers controlling the direction of the advance with their magnetic compasses, alert and making few mistakes. The prospect of Route 41, where a call from one of the telegraph poles which lined it could well bring up trucks from Dien Bien Phu to carry them the rest of the way in comfort, had its effect. Even the litter-bearers did not seem to want the hourly five-minute rest but were nervous and impatient when Schirmer gave the order to fall out.

Schirmer tried to impose the veterans' tried rules of caution and systematic checking of the terrain, but in the end even he had given up and allowed the march to progress at unaccustomed speed. The colonel was sick of the jungle, too; heartily sick of it and eager to get to base, clean up, have an ice-cold beer and sleep as he had never slept before.

Thus, he and the rest of the veterans overlooked the signs – the pressed-down patches of elephant grass, the dying odour of *nuoa-man*, the vine too artfully draped along the lower branches of the trees, the sudden silence of the jungle birds, as if high above the sweating men toiling below in the thick underbrush they were waiting expectantly for what had to happen.

'*Eile mit Weile*.'* White Lightning snapped the German phrase more than once, perhaps the only Headhunter not to be caught by the infectious mood of the battalion. But no one listened. If they listened to anything at all, it was Schulze's lip-smacking account, punctuated by delighted grunts, of what the Saigon slits were to expect when Mrs

---

*Roughly, 'hurry slowly.'

Schulze's sex-starved son was let loose upon them. They hastened to their date with destiny.

Captain Napalm heard the noise they made as they came ever nearer the road. He nodded to the under-lieutenant in charge of the bamboo bombs, who knelt and took hold of the cunningly concealed end of cord which was linked to the charges buried in the innocent-seeming bamboo groves that lined the opposite side of the road. 'Cadaver sticks,' he hissed from behind his mask. A group of Volunteers started planting the sharpened pegs in the ditch, carefully holding the clean end which had not been poisoned by being buried with dead bodies. If the French managed to get through the bamboo they'd stumble straight into the poisoned stakes.

'Wire,' he ordered.

'Fifty metres away, a wiry, half-naked Volunteer started to clamber up the telegraph pole to snip the wire above. In a few moments the spot would be cut off from any help. Napalm nodded his satisfaction. The spot was perfect, and the French, obviously believing that they were safe now after the abortive ambush, which had been a necessary sacrifice to lull them into the necessary mood of unconcern, were marching straight into the trap. He waved his good hand. As one, his veterans ducked under cover, holding their hands over the wet muzzles of the hounds which had led them here. All was ready.

Mercier held up his hand. The jeep-driver braked. Behind it the half-track clattered to a stop. Mercier stood upright and focused his glasses on the paddy fields. The sun was already beginning to burn the water into a haze and the peasants driving the oxen seemed to be ploughing through an expanse of cotton-wool which buried them up to their thighs. It was a peaceful, rural scene he had viewed half a hundred times in these last years, yet somehow something about it was wrong. Why were there so many men about and hardly a woman to be seen? Usually the man drove the beasts, but the hard work of tending the shoots under water, a back-breaking task at the best of times, even before the mosquitoes descended upon the fields, was usually left to the women.

'Anything the matter, Colonel?' Lequen inquired from the half-track to which Mercier had ordered him.

'Don't like it, Lequen,' Mercier snapped, lowering his glasses. 'Don't like it one bit . . . I'll push on ahead. You follow with the other jeep and half-track. If I draw fire, you know what to do?'

Lequen tugged his black patch and gave him a half-smile. 'Yes, Colonel, I vaguely remember.'

Mercier sat down at his driver's side. He drew his pistol and laid it on his lap, ready. 'You may advance,' he ordered. 'Keep it nice and slow. but if the shit starts to fly – '

Duclos swallowed and finished the sentence for him – he'd heard it often enough in the past – 'Go like a bat out of hell!'

'Exactly, my dear Corporal. Now advance.'

A worried Duclos let out the clutch and advanced.

'Perhaps another five hundred metres . . . perhaps another five hundred metres . . .' the information came down the happy column, relayed from mouth to mouth from the cartographers up at point.

'I'm so horny,' Schulze chortled, 'that I could pole-vault from here to Saigon, comrades.'

'Horny,' Pansy Petersen simpered. 'How absolutely marvellous! I simply don't know how you do it, Sergeant Schulze, what with the obnoxious food and the naughty old Slant-eyes and everything.'

'Well, let me put it like this, Lieutenant,' Schulze boasted grandly, while tired grins crossed the faces of his sweating listeners. 'If my grey-haired old mother – bless her soul – met me at this moment up there on Route 41, there could be a most embarrassing accident, I'm *that* horny!'

Schirmer, up now behind the cartographers, who were beginning to direct the point through the thick clumps of bamboo which barred their way, grinned, too. In spite of everything they had been through this last week, the men were in good form. Once back in Saigon, he'd ensure that they all got leave and see that the battalion's funds and whatever they could sell on the black market paid for the traditional orgy. He thought of the high-breasted Saigon whores, the best in the whole of South-East Asia, and licked parched lips in anticipation. He'd find himself a hotel of the de luxe class, he told himself, select two of the most beautiful whores he could afford, order two cases of champagne and retire to bed with them for the next forty-eight hours. What was the old crack the Headhunters always made to the whores before they took them upstairs? *'Have a good look at the floor, my little rabbit, because you'll be looking at the ceiling with yer legs spread apart for the next three days!'* Schirmer grinned again. Ten more minutes and they'd have broken through to Route 41. With the news he had to relate to General Navarre, he didn't doubt they'd all be back in Saigon within twenty-four hours. Saigon –

His sexual reverie was cut short by the high-pitched burr of several grease-guns in the bamboo ahead. In an instant the air was full of screams of pain and yells of anger. A storm of bullets rattled like heavy summer hail on the leaves all around. *'Tien Lien . . . Tien Lien . . .* Soldier, you die!' the frightening screams of hate rang out on all sides. The chilling waves of hoarse, exultant, vindictive fury turned Schirmer's blood to ice and his legs to jelly. For what seemed an age, he could not move while to his front his men started going down everywhere, threshing around in the dry bamboos in their agony. Then the stick grenades sailed through the air to burst between him and the cartographers. The first went down, his legs ripped off. The second's head was blown off and rolled away like a carelessly abandoned ball, while his body slumped against a bamboo and remained propped up there, a bloody horror.

The fate of the two cartographers awoke Schirmer to his own danger. They had walked slap-bang right into a beautiful ambush! There was no time for complicated tactics now. In cases like this, there was only one tactic: to charge straight into the enemy's automatics. They were the weapons which caused most casualties. If the Headhunters didn't knock those out and bogged down, the Slant-eyes would be able to massacre them at their leisure, picking them off one by one.

'*Headhunters*,' Schirmer bellowed above the ever-increasing lethal fury, '*follow me!*'

Gripping his grease-gun tightly to his right hip, he raced forward, springing over the bodies of dead and dying Headhunters, straight into the bamboos. Behind him his cheering men followed. Something caught his feet. He flew full-length on his face in the same instant that the trip wire signalled the waiting Slant-eyes. He pulled the cord cunningly draped through the bamboos. In one great, crazy roar, the earth erupted underneath the Headhunters charging furiously forward past their prostrate CO. Yellow light flashed blindingly. Men trying to keep their balance as the earth shook like a live thing threw up their arms to protect their eyes. Too late. They were sailing through the air, a whirling mass of severed limbs and mangled bodies.

The roar seemed never-ending. It reverberated back and forth ear-splittingly until finally it died away, to be replaced by the calls, screams and moans of the wounded and dying.

'*My goddam leg is blown to shit . . . SANITATER* . . . My shitting guts are ripped open . . . SANITATER . . . Oh, my Christ, my tail, they've blown my tail off . . . SANITATER . . . Don't give me any morphine, I don't want to go out . . . I've got it, right through the eggs . . . S A N I T A T E R . . .*'

Groggily Schirmer staggered to his feet, blood pouring in thick black streams from his nose and ears with the blast. His legs theatened to buckle underneath him at any moment. He blinked his eyes several times, as if trying to wake up from a deep sleep. The red mist cleared away. A metre in front of him a young blond Headhunter lay, still conscious but with his severed left foot still inside its jungle boot lying between his outstretched legs, his guts were ripped open, allowing blood and faeces to ooze out, and his right hand was a meaty mass of twisted, gory flesh and bones from which blood jetted in a thick, scarlet stream. Weakly Schirmer bent and tried to stop the flow by thrusting his fingers into the deep wound.

---

*Medical orderly.

'Knock it shitting off, sir,' the youngster said without any rancour in his voice. 'I'm gonna croak anyhow. Get the others out of this awful shit.'

It seemed to take Schirmer a long time to understand what the boy was saying. Gently the dying man pushed away the blood-soaked fingers from the wound. 'The others, sir,' he repeated.

Schirmer shook his ringing head. 'Rally . . . Rally on me,' he croaked. 'Forward . . .'

The survivors, staggering forward like sleepwalkers, commenced the second attack on the road.

The barefoot peasant stared at them open-mouthed as if he had never seen a white man or a jeep before. Suddenly he lobbed the fat, juicy melon he was holding across the road and ducked.

'*Mine!*' Mercier roared.

Duclos twisted the wheel. The jeep skidded to one side in the same instant that the melon exploded. The jeep's windscreen smashed into a cracked spider's web of broken glass. Next moment the little vehicle slammed into the ditch, its engine on fire. Mercier grunted and heaved the unconscious Duclos out of the driver's seat, dumping him in the stagnant green water of the ditch. Slugs scythed the air above his kepi. Mercier did not seem to notice. His pistol still stuck in his belt, he barked into the walkie-talkie, 'Well, Lequen, don't just hang on up there like a virginal schoolmarm waiting to spread her legs! Get on up here at the double and toast the eggs off these slant-eyed bastards. Do you – '

The rest of his words were drowned by the chatter of machine-gun fire and the sound of barefeet doubling across the road. He whipped out his pistol. Only twenty metres away, two peasants were running towards him under the cover of the machine-gun, hooked, woodsman's axe raised.

Mercier didn't turn a hair. Taking aim as calmly as if he were back on the range in Saigon, he pressed the trigger. The pistol jerked upwards. The leading Vietnamese skidded to a stop, his knee-cap smashed. He dropped the next instant. Mercier grunted something and fired again. The slug hit the Vietnamese in the centre of his face. It disappeared as if someone had just thrown a handful of red jam at it. He hit the road with a thud and didn't move again. Mercier was taking no chances. He pumped four carefully aimed slugs into the bodies, noting with pleasure how they jerked with the impact each time; then he whipped out the empty magazine, slapped in a new one and waited.

He didn't have long to wait. Led by the jeep the half-track bore down the road in a cloud of glaring white dust, its armour plating rattling as if it might fall off at any moment. Mercier sprang to his feet, dragging up the unconscious Duclos by the collar. The half-track howled to a stop, the machine-gunners standing in the cab next to the driver swinging .50 machine-guns from left to right, spraying the paddy field to both sides with bullets. Willing hands hauled the two men aboard.

'Off we go again!' Mercier yelled above the roar of the machine-guns and the frightened driver gunning his engine in case it stalled. 'Schirmer and his Boche are catching a packet up there. You, Lequen, take over that pea-shooter yourself.'

'Sir!' Lequen elbowed the pale-faced Legion gunner out of the way and sprang behind the half-track's terrible weapon as it set off once more, the slugs from the enemy in the paddy fields rattling off its metal sides like heavy tropical rain. Hastily he prepared it for action, knowing that he only had enough fuel for three 'shots'. If the Slant-eyes didn't run by then, they'd be in the shit, right up to their necks.

'*A moi!*' a bleeding Schirmer croaked as he stumbled through the charred, smashed bamboos, filled with the horribly mutilated Headhunter dead. '*A moi!*'

The survivors followed, taking ever more casualties as the triumphant enemy poured a vicious hail of fire at them from their cover on the other side of the road. White Lightning, just behind Schirmer, yelled with pain and sat down suddenly, holding his smashed right knee-cap. '*Shit . . . shit . . . shit . . .*' he cursed, as the others straggled by him, firing as they advanced. The first men emerged from the bamboos and ran straight into the cadaver sticks. Their screams drowned the chatter of the Slant-eyes' machine-guns. Men went down everywhere howling with pain, trying to ease their feet from the razor-sharp stakes which had cut right through their canvas jungle boots.

'*Down . . . for Chrissake, keep down . . .*' Schirmer ordered as he sprang across the ditch, filling with trapped men who were forgetting in their agony the stream of tracer cutting the air just above their heads. He dropped to his knees on the road and swung a burst from right to left. Now he could see the Slant-eyes in the trees everywhere, only a matter of metres away.

Schulze dropped on one knee next to him on the road, blazing away too. 'It's no good, sir,' he gasped, his great chest heaving with the effort, blood running down the side of his sweat-lathered face. 'They've got us by the short and curlies. We've got – '

'Must go on,' Schirmer sobbed, knowing that his battalion would be slaughtered if he didn't silence those automatics to the front. 'Got to go on.'

He rose to his feet, the bullets striking up vicious spurts of dust all around him, and began to totter forward again. Every single Viet seemed to concentrate his fire on the lone officer. Five metres . . . seven . . . ten . . . He had nearly done it.

The slug caught him low in the gut. He staggered, as if he had been struck by a gigantic fist. Behind him a low awesome groan came from Schulze. Schirmer tottered on a few steps, his knees buckling under him; his intestines began to slip through the blood-soaked fingers now clutched tightly to his ripped-open stomach.

'*Sir!*' Schulze cried desperately.

'*For –* ' The cry died on Schirmer's lips. He pitched forward, flat on his face, and lay absolutely still.

'*The officer!*' Captain Napalm screamed in a sudden, frenzied excitement as the enemy colonel pitched to the ground. 'Concentrate on the officer!'

His triumphant Volunteers needed no urging. Half a hundred weapons concentrated on the prostrate officer. Slugs cut the air around him everywhere. The bodies of his dead troopers jumped time and time again as bullets struck them. Schulze, attempting to crawl to drag Schirmer to the cover of the ditch, buried his head in the dirt helplessly, lead striking the ground all about him.

'Hit him . . . *hit him!*' Napalm urged, knowing that they didn't have too much more time, already half-aware of the clattering tracks racing up the road from the direction of the paddy fields. His men redoubled their efforts.

Schulze fumbled for his last smoke grenade. He knew he couldn't make his CO's body, but at least the grenade might provide some cover. He grabbed the pin and heaved. The bomb exploded just to the other side of Schirmer's motionless body. It threw out a thick white screen of smoke.

Napalm rose to his feet. '*Bugler*,' he cried, '*sound the attack!*'

The frightened boy raised his instrument, in the same moment that the half-track careened around the corner. It braked with a hellish scream as the driver took in the scene: the body half-hidden by smoke, the triumphant Slant-eyes and beyond, gaunt and sinister in his black pyjama-like suit, their masked commander. Lequen reacted at once. He pressed the trigger of his terrible weapon. There was the sound of what might have been some fabled monster drawing in a huge breath. Next moment there was the searing hiss of flame as the flame-thrower fired. The bright burning tongue of fire reached out, lapped itself greedily around a group of Viets crouched in a tree firing, hid their screaming, hideously contorted faces from view for one long instant and then vanished to leave them rigid and fixed there in the skeletal smoking branches like monstrous dead blackbirds.

Napalm cringed. He remembered that terrible day with the French bomber coming out of the bright blue summer sky straight at him, bearing its hellish cargo of liquid fire, and prevented himself from screaming out in terror just in time.

Lequen swung the long ugly weapon round and fired again. Once more the huge hissing sheet of flame shot out. A group of Viets rushing for cover disappeared in it. When they reappeared they were reduced to crouching, charred pygmies.

Napalm had had enough. He could not stand any more of that terrible weapon. 'Bugler,' he gasped, fighting back the green bile which filled his throat nauseatingly, 'sound . . . sound the retreat . . .'

One minute later they were withdrawing into the trees, fighting to conquer their panic, only their officers' automatics preventing them from breaking and fleeing in wild disorder. They left behind them the road covered in dead Headhunters and the still, silent body of their commander, Colonel Erwin Schirmer . . .

Three: Rescue

ONE

There was no sound in the hot, high, elegant room save for the soft whir of the roof-fan which did little but stir the air. Outside the noise of Saigon's afternoon traffic was muted by the oppressive heat, and even General Navarre's spoilt cat seemed subdued and without energy.

Colonel Mercier waited, looking at Navarre's haughty, hook-nosed face and wondering if the white-gloved shit would ever respond to his statement. Half a battalion of his Boche massacred, Slant-eyes on Route 41 and Schirmer's dramatic information – yet it had taken him the best part of a day to work his way up the chain of command at HQ and when he had finally managed to get in to see Navarre, the general had taken the report without so much as a mild expletive in response.

General Navarre lit a cigarette carefully and placed it in the ivory holder. 'I suppose these Boche of yours, Mercier, can be trusted?' He began slowly breathing out smoke, hollowing out his narrow, vain mouth to form a ring. 'I mean, one hears so many tales of the Viets trying to suborn them these days.'

'Colonel Schirmer has been fighting the Reds since 1941, General. Although Moscow thinks he is dead, there is still a price on his head, dead or alive, in Russia. I hardly think he is the kind of man who would do a deal with Uncle Ho, sir.'

'I suppose not. But one can never be too careful, can one.'

'One can't,' Mercier mimicked him, but the effect was lost on General Navarre.

'So according to these tame Boche of yours, Ho and Giap are building a road through the Thai Mountains over the Red River and into the delta. But to what purpose?'

'Dien Bien Phu,' Mercier snapped. 'It's as plain as the big nose on my kisser.' He was deliberately crude, and he deliberately missed out the 'sir'.

Again Navarre did not seem to notice. 'Dien Bien Phu,' he laughed softly and fondled his cat. 'Hardly likely, don't you think? After all, it *is* my strongest garrison in the north.'

'Exactly, sir. That's why they'll attack it. They'll force a showdown. That Giap is a kind of Indo-Chinese Napoleon. He is vain, cruel and capable. He even tries to ape the Corsican in his use of artillery. He has no time for guerilla tactics like the rest of the Slant-eyes. His vanity can only be satisfied by the great set-piece battle – and, naturally, the great victory. Dien Bien Phu offers him exactly that – *sir.*'

'A yellow Napoleon – how utterly quaint, Mercier.' Navarre's face lost its soft smile and he stopped stroking the cat. 'Aerial reconnaissance confirmed the road early this afternoon.'

Mercier's face lit up. 'Didn't I tell –'

Navarre held up his hand for silence and Mercier stopped short. 'So he has his road and, as you rightly point out, our major fortified hedgehog in the north is Dien Bien Phu. All right, assuming he attacks it in his desire for a set-piece battle and prestige, as you have mentioned, what can he do, Mercier?' He shrugged eloquently. 'What can his barefoot hordes do against troops in entrenched positions, armed with tanks, planes and artillery? Tell me that, Mercier.'

'The survivors of the Special Para report they saw Russian-built trucks on the secret highway, towing 57mm cannon.'

'Good, then I'll give you that our mini-Napoleon might bring up small calibre cannon, but our positions are deeply entrenched. As long as we've got the air-strips, let them dominate the ground around the fortress; we can still bring in troops, supplies and the like.'

Mercier kept control of himself with difficulty. Navarre simply wouldn't see a position different from his own.

There was not a gram of flexibility about the man; he might well have been of the generation of 1940: hidebound generals who had lost France the war and nearly her empire, too. He bent down and reached into the brief-case lying between his highly polished riding boots. He unclipped it and brought out the object he had taken out of Schirmer's blood-stained pack before they had carried him to the half-track, with Schulze sobbing like a child at his side and holding his beloved CO's limp, pale hand.

'Now then, Mercier,' Navarre said with fake heartiness, 'what new little surprise have you got me?'

'*This*!' Mercier slammed the bright gleaming shell down on Navarre's antique desk making the cat jump with fear.

Hastily Navarre reassured it with, 'It's all right, my dear . . . all right.' He stroked it rapidly and lovingly. 'Now what's this, Colonel Mercier?'

'A shell – twenty-millimetre calibre to be exact – of Russian manufacture.'

'I might have spent years of my military career on the staff, Mercier, but I do manage to recognise a shell when I see one. What, pray, is so particular or special about this one?'

'It is meant for a 20mm quadruple flak cannon and it was found by the Special Para Battalion on a group of Chinese porters – suspected Red Army gunners – caught by my Boche in a village on the other side of the Red River.'

Navarre leaned across the desk, the cat forgotten now. He was not that hidebound; he knew the significance of the information. 'Go on, Mercier, what do you make of it?'

Mercier hesitated. Half-an-hour ago Navarre's Chief-of-Staff had laughed in his face when he had mentioned his suspicions, and he had just prevented himself from punching the fellow's fat face in time. 'Well, sir, Chinese Red Army gunners, flak ammo, and a secret highway – put them all together and you get this. Giap knows that the only real way to put Dien Bien Phu out of commission is to knock out the landing strips. He has no fighters of his own to do that, but if he had flak guns around –'

'Impossible,' Navarre interrupted him loudly, the look in his eyes clearly indicating that Mercier had shaken him. 'Quite impossible! So they might be bringing up flak, but not for Dien Bien Phu. Our planes would blast them off the face of the earth before they ever got them into position – '

'They're masters of camouflage. That road was hid – '

Navarre was not even listening. He spoke as if he were trying to convince himself. 'No, those guns – if they *do* exist – are intended to be emplaced to protect this secret highway of theirs. They knew we'd find it in due course – in fact, we've found it already, haven't we – and would start bombing it as we have done all their other supply routes. This time they think they're going to try a new trick on us – their own air defence. But I tell you, Mercier – '

He stopped abruptly. The doors had been flung open without even a knock. Navarre flushed. 'What the devil do you mean, sir?' he snapped, as the fat, well-fed Chief-of-Staff burst into the room.

'*Sales cons*,' he cursed. '*Les sales cons*!'

'What do you mean? Explain yourself!'

The fat Chief-of-Staff dabbed a streaming, worried brow with an elegant lace handkerchief. 'Please forgive me, General – '

'Get on with it, General!' Navarre thundered.

'Well, sir. I've got bad news . . . very bad news.'

Mercier tensed.

'Yes?'

Again the Chief-of-Staff dabbed his brow. 'Sir, I beg to report.' He made a pathetic attempt at drawing in his fat gut and standing at attention.

'*Nom de Dieu*!' Navarre cried in exasperation.

'The Vietnamese under General Giap commenced attacking Dien Bien Phu in strength one hour ago.' The Chief-of-Staff swallowed hard, his voice sinking as if to his shining boots. 'They're using . . . heavy artillery . . .'

Mercier did not even feel a sense of triumph. It was already too late. General Giap, the Yellow Napoleon, had beaten them!

TWO

The noise was tremendous. A Headhunter was making love to a whore on the window-sill of the hotel room with a cigar in his mouth and a bottle of beer in his hand. Both were naked. Down below the delighted French recruits cheered enthusiastically. Another naked whore was giving an NCO a Vietnamese massage, walking up and down the length of his back to the accompaniment of his grunts and groans, pausing each time to bend down and pull his toes till they popped. In a tin bath-tub in the corner a Headhunter, still wearing his helmet but otherwise naked, was being washed under water by a grinning, gold-toothed whore; his eyes were already beginning to pop from his head at her touch. The whole suite smelt of beer, sweat and sex.

'I told this slit, Schulzi, you've got a tail a metre long plus a tongue of fifty centimetres,' a grinning, crimson-faced NCO, his brawny arms encircling two naked whores, yelled across the packed room at a morose Schulze. 'Now try and live up to that one!'

Schulze did not respond; his face remained as glum as ever. 'You want good time . . . velly good time . . . number one time,' the plump little whore next to him crooned. 'Jiggy-jig, General. I give you something new.'

'Yer, leprosy!' Schulze cracked sourly, breaking free from her importuning hand which was already busy unbuttoning his flies. He walked away, forcing his way through the press, to the mountain of glistening beer bottles lying on a small iceberg of chipped ice and, picking one up, absently bit off the metal cap.

His mind was not on the Headhunters' traditional Saigon orgy. He could understand the single-minded desire of the survivors of that treacherous ambush on Route 41 to get bombed and laid. Normally he was the leader in such pursuits. But today his heart was not in it. His mind kept slipping back to that underground operating theatre at Dien Bien Phu, where the terribly wounded Headhunters were piled up in the corridors, groaning and moaning on their blood-filled, green stretchers; with everywhere the stink of urine, faeces, ether, sweat – and death.

Personally he had carried out four stiffs – each with massively swollen purple faces, mouths open like stranded fish, split tongues protruding upwards, bloody fluid trickling from their nostrils and rigor mortis holding their dead arms in front of them in an absurd frog-like position – to make room inside for the CO. Finally the medics had brought the colonel to where the half-naked surgeons worked – up to their knees in severed limbs – slicing, cutting and sewing under the glaring arc lights.

The whole length of Colonel Schirmer's naked body glistened in sweat. His eyes were wide open and his stare was directed straight ahead, but he saw nothing. Once he threw back his head and his white gritted teeth parted as if he were trying to speak, to curse, to cry. A spasm of intolerable pain wrenched the muscles of his face into a mask that hid the grinning skeleton beneath. His chest heaved rapidly. The hole in his taut stomach allowed the steady snake of red and brown, blood and faeces mixed, to spill onto the stretcher. Then Schulze had been ushered out to where the sweating orderlies were dressing the minor wounds of the survivors and he had squatted there numbly, unfeelingly, while a corporal had cut through the flesh of his wounded hand with a pair of shears.

Now, as Schulze stared at his bandaged white paw, he knew with all that in his memory he could drink the mountain of beer before him empty and still would not be able to get drunk. He made up his mind. He grabbed his kepi and, ramming it firmly on his shaven skull, left the crazy room unnoticed. '*Screw the world*,' the Headhunter making love to the whore on the window-sill cried exuberantly. '*Screw the whole shitting world*!'

Aimlessly Schulze wandered through the congested streets of Saigon. Horn blowing substituted for traffic policemen. Beautiful girls in *ao dais* smiled at him from doorways and formed a circle with their forefingers and thumbs. He hardly noticed. Old women with gold-toothed grins tried to sell him dirty pictures. He pushed them away. Little boys grabbed at his trousers and tried to sell him 'number one cherry sister'. He dragged himself free, his mind full of the underground hospital and the sweating Sengalese orderlies bundling up the Headhunters who had died on the operating tables into green sacks and thrusting them into the long, narrow ice-boxes, as if they were laying down meat for a hard winter.

His aimless progress through the capital was held up by an old woman and a barefoot coolie with a squealing pig slung from the carrying pole held on their shoulders. Opposite in an open-front store, hung with traditional banners in Chinese, a group of squatting men were play-ing the scissors game, shouting at each other in Chinese as they shot out their fingers – two for 'stone', five for 'scis-sors'; the latter always winning against stone because their blades broke on it.

'Stupid shits,' someone said in French at his side, 'play-ing shitting kids' games like that when the roof's falling in on the shitting Slope-heads.'

Schulze turned slowly. A drunken, barrel-chested sergeant 1st class of the Legion stood swaying there un-steadily, his starched khaki chest ablaze with medal rib-bons, including the *Croix de Guerre*.

'You German?' he grunted in his own language.

The NCO nodded, his faded blue eyes red with drink. '*Jawohl, SS – the Bodyguard*.'

Routinely Schulze held out his good hand. '*SS Wotan*,' he muttered.

'Good mob that,' the drunk said, slurring his words.

'Fair,' Schulze agreed and joined the other man as he pushed his way through the strollers, jabbing his scarred elbow into anyone, French or Vietnamese, who took too long getting out of his path.

'Wet-arsed civvies,' the other man grumbled. 'But their day's coming, mark my words, comrade. They'll go hop one day, the whole shitting lot of 'em!'

Schulze took his mind off the Headhunters' dead and Colonel Schirmer, lying seriously wounded, perhaps even dead by now, in far-off Dien Bien Phu. 'What did you say?' he asked without much interest, pushing aside the barefoot little girl who was trying to undo his flies and begging for money with her free hand.

'The day of reckoning is coming, comrade, that's what I said,' the NCO replied with drunken seriousness. 'These Slant-eyes have had it too good since '45, getting fat on the blood of us poor shitting stubble-hoppers. Now they're going to find out what it's like when the crap starts flying around yer turnip.'

'How do you mean?'

The drunken NCO paused in the middle of the pavement, not even noticing the Vietnamese who bumped into his broad back, upsetting the overflowing chamber pot he was carrying to manure his kitchen garden down the front of his clothes. 'Haven't you heard, comrade? Uncle Ho's happy hooligans have started a big new offensive up north – the shits.'

Schulze's absent look vanished. 'Where?' he demanded, suddenly alarmed.

'Oh,' the drunk swung his arm out carelessly, knocking the kepi off an officer, who flushed crimson and opened his mouth to bellow an order but then looked at the two giant NCOs and changed his mind, 'up there in the delta some place.'

Schulze grabbed hold of the drunk's shirt and pulled him up tightly to his own broad chest. 'Where exactly?' he snarled, forgetting the pain in his hand. 'Out with it, shitmouth!'

'Dien Bien Phu. They started pounding it with artillery five hours ago . . . Hey, what about a beer and a bit o' slit, comrade,' he yelled, but Schulze was already pounding across the street, ignoring the honking horns and screeching of brakes as he raced for the taxi-rank.

THREE

Carefully, very carefully, White Lightning removed his plastered leg from the complicated pulley arrangement above the white metal cot and swung himself gingerly onto the shaking floor. The orderlies were already busy at the hellishly noisy helicopter pad behind the underground hospital, carrying in new casualties from the outlying forts, and would have no eyes for him. Hopping on his good leg, he began to make his way down the cramped corridor, pausing at every second bed to catch his breath. Here and there a less-seriously wounded Headhunter recognised the second-in-command and made some comment. White Lightning forced a wan smile and told himself that whatever happened at Dien Bien Phu, he was going to get his Krauts out; the guys deserved the best.

He passed 'Graves', piled high with dead soldiers of all races clasped together indiscriminately and stinking to high heaven. He wrinkled up his nostrils with disgust and told himself the orderlies ought to get them on ice before the rats which now lurked everywhere in the corridors scented them.

He hobbled through the lines of new wounded, who lay naked on stretchers outside the operating theatre, groaning and moaning while they waited their turn, some of them giving off the stench of burnt flesh.

He paused and looked in at the operating theatre, crowded with wounded being worked on under the glaring arc lights. In the number one position, two doctors were administering closed cardiac massage on a flaccid, skinny boy with multiple wounds, the vigorous chest compression making his ribs crack audibly. At number two, a gigantic naked Sengalese lay, his black body glistening with sweat, his flaccid penis drooped across his muscular thigh, his head wrapped tightly in a blood-soaked white bandage, his breath coming in grunting snorts. He was unattended and White Lightning knew why; his brain was

hopelessly damaged – he would die anyway. On the third
operating table, two orderlies were fighting to hold down
a young officer, who was screaming with his eyes tightly
closed, '*Ho, Ho, Ho, Ho, Sack Ho, Hate Ho, Fuck Ho,
But don't talk to Ho*,' while an angry, sweating surgeon,
naked to the waist, was attempting to snip off what was
left of his right leg with a pair of shears.

White Lightning swallowed hard and hobbled on, trying not to see the mangled limbs on all sides and hear the
grunts and groans, followed by their eerie jingle, '*Ho . . .
Ho . . . Ho . . .*' It died finally as the bunker heaved and
swayed like a ship running into a sudden hurricane as
another salvo of heavy shells straddled the place, forcing
the dust out of the cracks in the ceiling like grey rain.

White Lightning hopped to the exit. Outside there was
the blare of white light on the horizon. He ducked hurriedly. Another salvo straddled the fort, rocking it. Outside two huge mushrooms of smoke rose into the still blue
afternoon sky, almost obscuring the helicopter which
came clattering in to bring more wounded. '*Twelve . . .
eighteen . . . six . . .*' the loudspeaker just next to his head
in the sandbagged passage-way blared. Since yesterday
White Lightning knew what those code-words meant.
Stretcher cases, walking wounded, dead. They were
meant to keep the garrison confused as to the meaning.
He pressed himself against the wall, as the orderlies came
tumbling out to meet the dancing helicopter, their
uniforms pressed tightly against their bodies by the prop-
wash.

A minute later, they came doubling back with their
moaning, groaning, cursing burdens. '*My damn leg is
blown to shit . . . a land mine . . . Am I going to lose my
shitting flipper? . . . Ouch, ouch, ouch . . .*' And then the
silent ones: the dead.

White Lightning bit his bottom lip and took another
look at the flashes of the long-range artillery in the hills
and then at the smoking holes that dotted the landing strip
like the work of some monstrous mole. He had seen it all
before in the Big War; this was an all-out effort, just as the
CO had figured it would be. He remembered Bastogne in
that snow-bound December of '44 when the Krauts had
surrounded the little Belgian town and the weather had

been bad for three long days. Air had not been able to supply them; food and ammo had started to run out and morale had begun to break down fast, very fast. Within twenty-four hours, the cellars and foxholes inside the shot-up town had been full of 101st Airborne troopers who had seemingly bugged out from the front. Dien Bien Phu was so different. If that air strip outside went out of action, it would mean curtains. The Frogs would present the fortified hedgehog to the Slant-eyes on a silver platter.

Worried, grimacing every now and again as pain shot up his wounded leg, White Lightning started to hobble back the way he had come, pressing himself to one side every time the orderlies dashed back and forth on their errands of mercy, noting automatically that the corridors of the underground hospital were beginning to fill up more quickly than the surgeons could clear away the ever increasing number of casualties.

He hobbled by the stench of the lung-cases and on by the weird, frightening moans of the nut cases – the old Section Eight guys, as they had once called them in the Big War – then past the operating theatre again, where a Moroccan soldier with half his hand blown off was feeding the sweating surgeon water from his canteen as the doc sorted through the ragged stump of a blown-off leg attached to a screaming kid who didn't look more than sixteen.

'So this time the yellow, slant-eyed pricks have pissed off the wrong nigger!' a huge sweating Sengalese negro bellowed at him in atrocious French. 'Get me bandaged up and I'll tear the mothers apart, limb from limb.' The negro held up his bleeding stumps and began to cry, great tears rolling down his sweating coal-black face.

White Lightning dodged him and came to his destination, the little ward at the far end of the underground hospital reserved for field-grade officers. He pushed aside the curtain and entered. Two of its three occupants were unconscious or asleep, but Schirmer, his face a putty colour and with tubes inserted in his nose and attached to his arm that was linked to an overhead drip, flicked open his eyes at once. 'You,' he said weakly.

'Yes, Skipper. I'm really a general in disguise on a

secret inspection tour. I got my knee shot off so I could get in here.'

Schirmer smiled softly. 'I'd prefer a big blonde with secret tits,' he patted the side of his bed. 'Sit down. Take the weight off your feet, Major. Well?'

'Shitty, Skipper. Decidedly shitty.'

'Trouble up top?' Slowly, moving his head as if it were worked by ancient rusty springs, Schirmer indicated the ceiling which was shaking again under the impact of yet another salvo.

'Not yet. Plenty of incoming mail, of course. But so far they haven't registered correctly on the landing strip. But when they do – ' White Lightning whistled softly. '*Brother*!'

'How are my Headhunters, Major?'

'We took one hell of a beating. Fifty per cent casualties. Not much the medics could do for the poor guys who went into the bamboos. The mines played hell with them. But the wounded are coping OK.'

Schirmer nodded slowly, very slowly. 'How many of my boys are there in the dock?'

'Mercier took what was left of the battalion back to Saigon with him. I'd guess there must be about fifty of us here. One of the medics said they shipped out the lightly wounded as soon as the artillery barrage started. Mostly bed cases are left behind.'

Schirmer absorbed the information for a few moments. At his side one of the unconscious officers groaned piteously but fell silent again almost immediately. 'What a shitting mess,' he said at last. 'Caught like this when the shit really is flying!'

'Yeah, this time the shit has really hit the fan. Uncle Ho is making a max effort. Those cannon out there are not just harassment. Uncle Ho and his Slope-heads are going to take this place.'

Another salvo of shells emphasized his words. The underground room trembled. The wounded, unconscious French officer started up in bed with shock, his eyes still closed, then fell back again.

Schirmer waited until the noises of the shells exploding had subsided. 'Major, how's your knee?' he asked.

'I won't be running any long-distance races for a while,

but I'll survive, Skipper. Why do you ask?'

'Because I want you to check out the actual physical state of every Headhunter in this place.'

'Why?'

'Because we must be prepared to get out of here when the time comes,' Schirmer said baldly.

'Cripples like us – *out of here*?' White Lightning exclaimed incredulously.

'It's either that or death, Major. When this place surrenders or is stormed, which will be the case, I'm sure of it – after all, Giap's prestige is at stake – there's going to be no nice prison cage for the Headhunters with Red Cross parcels and visits from a neutral power. For us, there will be only one thing – *death*!'

White Lightning stared sombrely at Schirmer for a moment while the enemy guns thundered again outside. 'As soon as I can make it,' he said, 'I'll see Colonel de Castries about having the men evacuated, Skipper. We're only useless mouths to feed and take up space here. A couple of 6-47s and that would be that. If – '

The rest of his sentence was drowned by the explosion of shell nearby and the sudden, tremendously rapid firing of a much lighter cannon. The bunker shook. Next instance there was a huge crash and French orderlies were running down the corridor, crying. '*Helicopter down . . . Chopper bought it . . . All twelves . . . Helicopter down . . .*

White Lightning looked at Schirmer, aghast.

Schirmer nodded slowly, as if he had read the shocked American's mind. 'There'll be a little difficulty about those evacuation planes now, Major,' he said softly.

'That was flak,' White Lightning finally managed to get the words out in a strangled voice. 'The Slant-eyes are using flak cannon!'

'Yes, now we know what those coolies intended the 20mm shells for. Uncle Ho is going to cut Dien Bien Phu off from the air. Major, I think you'd better start arming the Headhunters . . . '

Colonel Schirmer then slumped back on his hard pillow, telling himself he had never felt lower in his twelve years as a soldier. He and his men were trapped and helpless.

Wordlessly, White Lightning hobbled out.

FOUR

General Giap lowered his binoculars, and the carpet of dead bodies outside the shattered fort over which now waved the black flag of the Revolution vanished from the circles of glittering, calibrated glass.

Standing next to him, gaunt, silent and frightening, Captain Napalm surveyed his commander. Giap's features were softly moulded, almost feminine, he couldn't help thinking, with the eyebrows like black feathers, but they did radiate an intelligent, calculating confidence. Even the tremendous losses of this day, when his 'human sea' heroes of the People's Army had been slaughtered by their thousands, had not shaken that confidence.

Giap turned and indicated that Napalm should follow him. For a few moments they walked together in silence, Giap watching where he put his small feet in the bloody mess of the battle-field, while everywhere in the twilight coolies trotted back and forth bearing the wounded survivors of the 312th Division's suicidal attack on *Beatrice*. Giap did not see them; he knew from the books of military history he had devoured when he had been a teacher at the *Lycée* that a great commander did not let his judgement be impaired by the sufferings of his men – and *he* was a great commander.

'Your Death Volunteers did very well this day, comrade,' he broke the heavy silence. 'They broke through the French wire at every spot assigned to them.'

'Thank you, Comrade General,' Napalm hissed from behind his mask, which stuck to his ruined face in the sticky evening heat.

'Tomorrow I will take *Fort Gabrielle* – a pretty name, isn't it, for a fort? – and then I shall isolate *Isabelle*.'

Napalm found the General's overweening confidence repugnant, but he continued to walk at his side in silence.

'Of course, the French will think I cannot keep taking

the casualties I will have to take in these attacks. They do not think that I can accept them. Unfortunately for them, however, they do not realise that I share the Great Mao's thoughts when he stated that "We can lose three hundred million killed and still win a war".' He gave Captain Napalm one of his cold little smiles.

'Yes, Comrade General,' Napalm said dutifully.

'Naturally I cannot take so many casualties. My regular divisions have a limited number of trained men. Once I have taken *Gabrielle* and isolated *Isabelle* and have knocked out their landing strip, then I will operate differently.' He paused and allowed a group of sweating coolies, their feet soaked red in blood from walking over the dead, carry by the limp bodies of the divisional commander of the 312th and his deputy. Giap did not even seem to notice them.

'How, Comrade General?' Napalm asked after they had resumed their walk.

'Like this.' He bent and picked up an abandoned bayonet. With it he scratched a circle in the dust. 'Dien Bien Phu.' He drew a line across the upper half of the circle. 'The outlying forts, which I will capture, as I have already stated, in the next few days.' Outside the remaining half of the circle, he scratched another one. 'Thereafter we shall resort to the tactics of the eighteenth century.'

'What do you mean, comrade?'

'We shall encircle the main French defence complex with a huge trench, thus,' he pointed to the line he had just drawn in the dust, 'and then sap inwards in the good old-fashioned way until we are ready to launch our final attack in full strength. Each day we will move a little farther, digging as we go. Naturally the French will counter-attack and attempt to fill our trenches in again. But they haven't the manpower we have.' He held out a well-scrubbed hand at the sweating coolies trotting by with their groaning human burdens. 'I have a million of those at my disposal.'

Inwardly Captain Napalm smiled. Giap, the 'Father of the People's Army', as he styled himself, was still a bourgeois, with the middle-class's contempt for the coolie.

'After a while we will retain the trenches and slowly close a ring of iron around the defenders. Once the landing strip is knocked out, there will be only one way into Dien Bien Phu – by parachute – and *no* way out.' Giap let this information sink in before he continued. 'Now, Comrade Napalm, in my opinion, the main centre of enemy resistance, after *Fort Isabelle* is isolated, will be *Huguette*.' He drew a mark in the circle. 'Here. It has the landing strip and their main hospital. It is my guess that it will become de Castries's HQ once the real battle commences. Comrade, it is going to be the task of your Death Volunteers to open the door to *Huguette* for my regulars.'

'How?' Napalm asked eagerly. The destruction of the enemy's main post in a great battle would be something worth dying for.

'Not by suicidal rushes as today, my dear comrade. No, not that way. I know you and your brave comrades are dedicated to death for the cause. But I must not waste your valuable lives for meaningless objectives. No, when you die, you die achieving something of value. Thus there will be no more charges against the wire and concrete fortifications for the Volunteers. You will go in underground.'

'A tunnel, Comrade General?' Napalm asked quickly.

'Exactly. I am going to place one thousand coolies under your command. As soon as I have drawn the ring of iron around the main fortifications they will start tunneling under your leadership.'

'To what point in *Huguette*?'

Giap frowned. 'I have given that problem some thought, comrade. The place is exceedingly well defended, with most of its works virtually underground. It would be very difficult to blast a way in through that depth of earth and concrete. However, it does have two *points d'appui*.* He used the French word, knowing that Napalm like himself had once studied in France in another age. 'Here to the front and the other one – here to the rear.' He dug the bayonet into the earth to indicate the location of the sally-ports. 'Now the second

---

*A kind of sally-port from which the defenders could launch a counter-attack from a covered position.

one seems to me to be the better from our point-of-view.
It is masked from the fort's main guns and offers some
dead ground over which you will launch your final attack
to gain an entrance for my regulars.' He gave Napalm
another of his cold smiles. 'Is that all clear to you,
Comrade?'

Giap's cold-blooded schoolmaster's style irritated the
man in the black mask. 'Perfectly, Comrade General.
And when do I launch my attack?'

'Before the monsoons start.' A sudden warmth crept
into the plump little general's voice. 'Napalm, on the first
of May I will launch my final attack. I must have that
sally-port by then. Victory before the monsoons come,
or – '

Giap did not complete his sentence. He didn't need to.
If he didn't take Dien Bien Phu before the fighting season
ended, his career as an Army commander would be over;
Uncle Ho would replace him. Napalm knew that.

Giap caught hold of the gaunt, masked soldier's
good arm. 'Napalm,' he pleaded, 'give me my place in
history . . .'

FIVE

'*Camerone Day, Legionnaires!*' the metallic voice taunted the men manning the parapets across the ruined waste of no-man's land. '*No wine, no special food for the Legion this day, eh? You bring your weapons and come across to us and we give you wine – and women, beautiful women . . .*'

'*And you can kiss my beautiful arse!*' an angry, weary legionnaire called back, using the same words their predecessors had said nearly one hundred years before when fifty of them had been besieged by over a thousand Mexicans.

His sally brought a ripple of tired laughter from his comrades. Somebody struck up the Legion's marching song, *Le Boudin*, and its bold words echoed across the battlefield of Dien Bien Phu.

'*You celebrate in hell now . . .*' the metallic voice called angrily and clicked off.

The Legionnaires sang on.

Another dawn broke over the fortress, grey and dirty. The night's customary fighting for the Vietnamese trenches had raised a fine black and red dust, which fell slowly like volcanic ash and obscured the hilltops, now shredded of all vegetation by the permanent bombardment. The wasted lunar landscape waited for another day of battle.

By this day, 30th April, Dien Bien Phu had been under siege for over a month. At the end of March the airstrip had been shelled permanently out of commission. One week later *Isabelle* had been cut off from the rest of the fortified hedgehogs and could only be communicated with by radio.

That first week of April, 1954, a fierce, bloody, air-to-ground duel had developed between the French Air Force and the besiegers' flak, manned by Chinese Red Army 'volunteers'. Seventy to eighty planes attacked the gun sites daily, but the Chinese gunners were constantly changing their positions and in the end they began to win. Navarre mustered the whole of the French air transport fleet, one hundred planes, to make a mass drop of supplies to a garrison which was down to one week's food and ammunition. They got through, with burning Dakotas going down on all sides, and the garrison was able to continue fighting.

By the middle of the month, Giap had 50,000 troops surrounding de Castries's remaining 12,000, many of them wounded more than once. But French morale was good. De Castries counter-attacked time and time again and inflicted terrible losses on the Viet Minh. But Giap could afford the losses. The Viet Minh swamped the defenders with their manpower, advancing into the muzzles of the French cannon until the bodies of their dead were piled high in the barbed wire, masking the fire of the defenders.

In the third week of April Giap completed his encirclement of the main fortifications, with his sweating coolies and troops, officers and men alike, sapping their way steadily forward so that General (he had received that star by parachute) de Castries, watching their progress from his bunker, was reminded of the trenches in France in the First World War. Now both sides lived underground during the day and fought at night. Nightly the bunkers filled up with the wounded and dying, with the dead being stacked up outside in great piles like ghastly logs of firewood, their rigid arms tied up inside their cartridge belts so that they were easier to transport. The sweating, half-naked surgeons worked in shaking rooms, up to their rubber boots in blood, sloshing it around them when they moved from one operating table to another, to the sounds of vomit, curses, cries and whimpers and to the stench of shit and blood. For twelve or more hours at a time they laboured until they collapsed over the operating tables. But the wounding and killing went on.

The first rains started, heralding the monsoons soon to come. French air supply was hindered and a worried General Navarre, knowing he would have to go if he lost Dien Bien Phu, hoped that it would hamper Giap's road supplies, too. It didn't. The Molotavas got through even

more quickly now that the enemy air force was no longer
bombing the secret highway. In despair he threw in his
last reserves: two Legion para battalions were dropped
under cover of darkness and made it to the forts without
too many casualties.

Steadily the Viet Minh worked their way ever closer to
the forts, digging and fighting, fighting and digging, urged
on by a relentless, fanatical Giap, out to beat the monsoons and to meet his deadline. The new paras made a
counter-attack. It failed. There would be no more.

On the 22nd April, the rains came. The dust bowl of
Dien Bien Phu was transformed into a sea of mud and
swamp. The Viet Minh started to plaster the French positions with the whole weight of their artillery. Day and
night the valley quaked with the roar of the guns. Nightly
the ridges all around blinked with angry red lights like the
maws of enormous blast furnaces. Shells of all calibres
ripped through the sky with hoarse, exultant screams.
The bunkers shook and heaved. The defenders huddled
there screaming, blood oozing out of their ears from the
blast. Now the grievously wounded flowed out into the
underground corridors everywhere and the serious cases
had to double up, two to a bed with more often than not a
less seriously wounded man stretched out on a blanket
underneath the bed.

The surgeons worked round the clock, kept going by
black coffee, cigarettes and|benzedrine; they ripped off
clothes, splintered shattered limbs, sliced them off, inserted drips and tubes, mechanically moving from one
tortured, mutilated body to another, their rubber gloves
stiff with matted blood, vomit, crap. No longer were they
hearing the pleas in half a dozen languages: '*You can save
my leg, Doc, can't you . . .? It hurts like shit. Gimme a shot,
quick, Doc . . . Help, Doc, I'm pissing blood . . .*'

Outside, the cowards, the would-be doctors, the holy
men volunteers of the Grave Registration Company,
bundled the gruesome, torn, blasted, mangled, destroyed
young human beings – black, brown, yellow, white –
into the green bags, zipped them up, attached the official
tag and then hosed away the blood, the faeces, the bits of
body and brains, as if to leave no trace that the stiffs had
ever existed.

Now it was the 30th April. Four of the original forts had fallen. The nearest Viet Minh positions were within five hundred metres of General de Castries's command post, with the mass of Giap's troops established between the cut-off *Fort Isabelle* and the remainder. A strange, ominous calm hung over the battlefield; it seemed to herald the storm soon to come.

'*The enemy attack on Huguette 6 commenced at 17.30 hours yesterday,*' the dry detached voice on the radio announced. '*According to official sources here in Saigon, its objective was the command post. The enemy succeeded in surrounding the post by midnight but an energetic counter-attack by our troops at zero four hundred hours this morning threw them back. Enemy repulsed with great casualties for slight losses on our part by dawn. Today the battlefield is reported quiet. It has been announced in Cannes that Miss Brigit Bardot –*'

'Turn that crap off,' Schulze snapped and took a long swallow of his warm beer, as if to wash down the unpalatable news of a kind he had been hearing for over a month now.

A Headhunter reached up and turned the radio off.

Schulze slung his empty beer bottle at the wall. It rattled down, trailing wetness after it. 'What a shitting Camerone Day,' he exclaimed in disgust. 'The CO and the Ami and fifty troopers cut off up there in Dien and only warm, three per cent gnat-piss beer to drink – on orders of his royal highness General Navarre!'

'I could have got you schnaps, Schulze,' Duclos volunteered from the corner. 'For a consideration.' The shortsighted hunchback made the Continental gesture of counting money.

'You worry about getting us out of Saigon when the time comes, cripple,' Schulze snorted. 'You would have thought that chief of yours Mercier would have thought of some way of pulling Colonel Schirmer and the rest out of Dien by now.'

The intensely loyal Duclos pulled a face. 'He tried. My God, how he tried! He pulled every string he knew. But General Navarre will not risk a single plane over

Dien that is not carrying essential cargo. Paris screams murder every time one of them goes down. They cost money – plenty of money.'

'Those pink pansies!' Schulze said scornfully.

'Careful, careful, Schulze,' Pansy Petersen said mildly, busily engaged in manicuring his delicately and discreetly varnished nails. 'You are talking of those I love.'

Nobody sniggered. Even the outrageous, homosexual officer couldn't shake off their mood of despair this rainy April day.

'Besides, the last time they tried to fly in a Red Cross plane,' Duclos continued, 'the Slant-eyes let it have all they had. Curtains for crew and passengers.'

Someone tossed Schulze another bottle of beer, and he pulled off the metal cap with his teeth. 'But we've got to do something. Dien is turning into another Stalingrad. If they don't get out soon, Uncle Ho'll slaughter 'em.'

'Yes, I agree entirely.'

The Headhunters shot to attention. A tired-looking Mercier stood at the open door, gleaming and elegant in his best uniform. He smiled softly and told them to sit down again.

'After all it is our day of celebration, comrades of the Legion, though I can't recollect a more unhappy one than this April 30th.'

'Any news, sir?' Petersen enquired, offering the little one-armed colonel a seat.

'Only the bad sort. Our beloved Commanding General,' Mercier could not hide the contempt in his voice, 'still maintains he can win at Dien Bien Phu, but the white-gloved gentlemen of the staff are already wagering about his probable successor.'

'And Colonel Schirmer?'

'I took the opportunity of the Camerone Parade to broach the subject.' Mercier shrugged bitterly. 'No hope. The Legion alone has over a thousand wounded inside Dien Bien Phu, which Saigon can't get out. General Navarre naturally is not prepared to risk a plane for my Boche, as he delights in calling them.'

'But we can't let Colonel Schirmer and the rest go under just like that, sir,' Schulze ventured boldly. '*We can't*!'

'We'll try anything, sir,' Petersen added his voice to Schulze's.

'There are two hundred or more of us, sir,' Schulze continued, 'just itching to have a crack at the Slant-eyes again. All we want is a plan and your approval.'

'By land possibly, sir?' Petersen suggested.

'Impossible, Lieutenant! The Vietnamese are everywhere in the delta. It would take you an age to fight your way through them and time is running out. It is my guess that Uncle Ho will make an all-out effort to take Dien Bien Phu before the monsoon starts. Thereafter, the weather will make it difficult to carry out any large scale operations. No, by land is out of the question.'

'We'll drop from the air, sir,' Schulze said eagerly. 'Without chutes, if necessary.' No one laughed at his desperate joke; they were all too intent and serious now.

Mercier shook his head. 'There are no more paras going into Dien Bien Phu. The order came from Paris itself and it is not too difficult to realise why. If – no, *when* – the garrison surrenders, Paris does not want the numbers to be too high.' He laughed bitterly. 'The Press would play it up and they might not get re-elected. No, Sergeant-Major, there will be no going in by air.'

A heavy silence fell on the dispirited Headhunters. From far away the blare of the trumpets and the thud of the big drum signalled another Legion parade and General Navarre's attempt to convince Saigon that all was normal when, in fact, his élite troops were fighting for their lives – and his career – in far-off Dien Bien Phu.

'Sir.' It was the little, bespectacled hunchback who broke the long silence.

All eyes turned slowly towards him as he squatted there, drinking his fizzy lemonade, for Corporal Duclos abhorred strong drink.

'Yes, Corporal?' Mercier said moodily.

'I have a little idea,' he began hesitantly, as if he were not sure of himself. 'You know those Americans, sir?'

'You mean the Flying Tigers?'

'Yessir, General Chennault's Chinese Air Transport Company. As you know, they work for hire – flying transports.'

Mercier nodded. Everyone in Saigon had heard of the

crazy American general, who before the war had flown for the Chinese against the Japanese with his civilian pilots. During the war he had been commissioned into the American Army, but he hadn't been able to settle down. Now for the last few years he had been flying as a mercenary with his mixed Chinese-American force for anyone who could pay him enough.

'Well, sir, last week, now that his men cannot fly the transports into Dien Bien Phu any more, he volunteered to take over the new helicopter gun-ships coming from America against the enemy – for a higher fee, naturally,' Duclos added in the manner of a man who appreciated the value of money.

'Naturally,' Mercier echoed, but the irony was wasted on Duclos.

'Well, you little crooked cripple, piss or get off the pot!' Schulze exclaimed impatiently. 'What have all these Amis got to do with us and Colonel Schirmer?'

'This. I have heard from my sources that these Americans will do anything for English whisky and white women. I've heard, too, that on the day after tomorrow they are to attack Viet positions in the jungle a few kilometres away from Dien Bien Phu. It is to be a kind of experiment with the new gun-ships.' He shrugged easily. 'At least it will please our American backers, if nothing else. Now if those crazy Americans could be provided with the English whisky and the white women they crave –'

'But that is impossible, Duclos,' Mercier snapped, already ahead of him. 'Whatever white women there are in Saigon are firmly in the hands of senior officers or married to the richer planters. As for whisky,' he rolled his eyes, 'our noble Commanding General treasures his more than he does his war plans.'

But Schulze and the rest of the Headhunters were already clambering to their feet. Mercier stared in amazement at their suddenly happy faces as they grabbed their kepis prior to leaving. '*What . . . where* are you going?' he stuttered, while behind him the bespectacled hunchback smiled his secret little smile of achievement.

'Where, sir?' Schulze bellowed happily, ramming his kepi down on his shaven bullet-head. '*Why, to find that Tommy firewater – and round-eyed slit . . .*'

SIX

The sentry never knew what hit him. The sock filled with sand struck him neatly, just behind his right ear. He relaxed his grip on his carbine and began to fall. Schulze caught him and lowered him almost tenderly to the gravel. He flashed a look to left and right. The noise of the party in General Navarre's villa must have drowned any noise they might have made. The way was clear. 'Come on, you banana-suckers. Let's get inside!'

Noiseless in their rubber-soled shoes, the little band of black-faced Headhunters in their stocking caps sneaked in through the door the sentry had been guarding. From further on up the long gloomy corridor there came the muted sound of laughter, clinking glasses and music.

Schulze was not interested in General Navarre's Camerone Day party; his mind was on the plan of the house that Duclos had provided them with. 'The cellars'll be to the right, beyond the kitchen. Follow me, *sharpish*!'

On their toes they crept by the open door of the kitchen, from which came the sound of bubbling pans and the heavy spiced odour of much garlic.

'White-gloved shits,' Schulze muttered to himself sourly. 'Our boys in Dien are eating canned shit and the officers of the staff feed their fat faces with the best, the shitehawks!'

They swung to the right. There was the cellar-keeper's room, where Duclos had predicted it would be. Schulze held up his two fingers and then pointed to the floor. Two of his little band peeled off and took up their posts at the entrance to the corridor, sandbags at the ready. Schulze waved the remaining men to follow him. Slowly, very slowly he opened the cellar-keeper's door. The Chink was sprawled on his bed, with his trousers off, reading a pornographic magazine. He looked up, startled. His mouth opened to shout. Schulze beat him to it. He grab-

bed him by the open shirt and hauled him from the bed so
that his feet trampled the air, pornographic magazine still
clutched in his soft hand. 'Listen, you dirty yeller Chink,'
he hissed in atrocious French. 'If you open yer kisser, I'll
saw the nuts off'n yer with a blunt bayonet. Now then, I'm
gonna let you down and one peep – '

The violently trembling Chinese stared round at the
dark faces and crossed himself hastily, 'Sengalee,' he
quavered. 'Lotten black men.'

'Yer, lotten black men,' Schulze mimicked the scared
man's inability to pronounce an 'r'. 'Now where's the key
to the lotten cellar?'

'But Genelal Na – '

Schulze made a threatening gesture, as if he were about
to draw out his bayonet. The Chinese grabbed the key
from the nail above his head. 'Key.' He thrust it into
Schulze's big paw as if it were red-hot. 'You take
evellythink.'

'Yer, I take evellythink. . . .'

Ten minutes later a silent line of black-faced men
emerged from the tradesmen's entrance, each man carrying a wooden case bearing the legend 'produce of Scot-
land', leaving behind them a prostrate Chinese who was
about to have a heart-attack . . .

'But I say, Schulze, what if we're caught?' *General* Pansy
Petersen protested sotto voce, as the ancient female trio
scraped away on a dais in the middle of Saigon's most
elegant café. 'They'll nail us to a cross!'

Colonel Schulze, his chest ablaze with ribbons he had
never earned, smiled winningly past the 'General' at a
bunch of rich planters' wives, working their way through a
mountain of cream cakes, pausing only to throw looks in
his direction and giggle sillily.

'They've got to catch us first,' Schulze whispered and
gaily tossed a hand-kiss in the French women's direction,
which caused them to giggle even more.

'Besides,' an unhappy Petersen protested, 'I feel so
dirty, perverted even. After all, they *are* women.'

'Imagine they're nice young boys,' Schulze rode rough-
shod over his objections. 'Now as soon as they strike up a
waltz, over you go with me and invite them to take their

fat cake-holes out of that cream and dance.'

'Oh my God, dance – *with a woman*!' Petersen protested miserably. 'If my friends ever get to know about this, I'll be ruined socially.'

'With all due respect, Lieutenant,' Schulze growled, 'I'll ruin yer personally if you don't stop running off at the mouth.'

On the dais, the leader of the trio, a skinny, grey-haired hag with her gold-rimmed spectacles attached to a chain which dangled down between her non-existent breasts, raised her bow with a flourish, crooked her elbow and, thrusting out her bony behind, started a waltz.

'Oh my Christ, she'll do herself an injury if she does that again!' Colonel Schulze said and rose. 'Come on, General. Turn on the charm.'

With a huge beam on his broad bronzed face, Colonel Schulze marched across the crowded café, neatly tripping up a slim Air Force captain who was hurrying towards the women's table, too, and giving a backwards jerk of his elbow into the plump stomach of a Paymaster Corps Major with the same intention. Together he and General Petersen bowed in front of the four women and kissed beringed, plump white hands all round to the delight of the planters' wives who knew they were a much sought after rarity in Saigon but who hadn't bargained with the attentions of a one-star general and a full colonel this dreary wet April evening.

'With your permission, my dear young ladies,' Schulze boomed in his best French to the two with whom they wouldn't dance this time, eyeing their ample charms with flattering, undisguised admiration, 'may we have the pleasure of the first dance with your delightful friends before you honour us as well?'

All attention, delicate hand-holding, attentive steering through the throng, bowing and cooing, the two Headhunters took their charges on to the floor to begin the waltz, with Schulze whirling the planter's wife around with so much élan and energy that she gasped, 'Ah, you Germans are so strong, so virile.' It, of course, prompted Schulze to push his knee between her legs and whisper, 'Ah, but my dear lady, what cannot we learn about love from you French flowers!'

'Charmer,' she simpered, trying to ignore the perspiration running down her powdered face – and something hard sticking into the base of her stomach.

The waltz gave way to a fox-trot; the fox-trot to a *java*. Coffee was replaced by champagne, champagne by cognac. The long rainy afternoon passed in a drunken, giggling, musical haze until the handsome and so youthful 'General' made his proposition: 'Giving a little party at my residence to a group of American officers. The servants will be sent away, of course. All very discreet.'

Schulze pressed his neighbour's plump, silk-stockinged thigh to emphasize just how discreet. She giggled. They all giggled. 'Plenty of bedrooms,' he explained, 'in case any one of you delightful ladies would happen to – er – get tired.' They giggled even more.

'Of course,' a red-faced, embarrassed 'General' Petersen said, 'you have my word of honour as an officer and gentleman that everything will be above board. The American officers, I believe, are all members of the Salvation Army, too.'

Schulze winked knowingly. They giggled uproariously.

Drunk, red-faced and still giggling, they staggered out of the café to where the stolen staff car bearing the star of a one-star general on its bonnet was waiting, with, to its rear, the truck laden with cases of looted whisky. Schulze clicked his fingers loudly.

Corporal Duclos shot out of the driving seat and stared open-mouthed at the giggling, drunken, planters' wives. He caught himself in time and thrust open the door for them.

'To the General's residence,' Schulze commanded grandly.

'At your service, Colonel.'

Schulze winked at him in the mirror and let his hand wander higher up the woman's plump thigh, telling himself that it was a waste of good slit, but it was all in a good cause. Half an hour later they halted at the American HQ. The young Yank officer who opened the front door breathed in awe at the sight of the women and the pile of whisky. '*Jesus H Christ, whisky galore and white gash! Now I can die happy!*'

The women giggled.

SEVEN

Delicately the pilot touched the vinegar-soaked bandage wrapped around his aching head and said for the third time, 'Some party! I'd forgotten what round-eyed slit looked like.'

Schulze nodded, though he did not understand a word. But the pilot's shaking hands before take-off and the fact that he had had frequent recourse to the oxygen flask indicated that the party with the giggling French women had been a success. Now he concentrated on the terrain ahead, over which the gun-ships, packed with as many Headhunters as they could cram into them, advanced towards the rebel-held area in a great, whirling, noisy V.

The view was magnificent over the whole rice bowl with its small, fat, lush-green fields and tiny straw and wood hamlets stretching to the far mountains, hidden in a haze that indicated that the monsoon could not be far off now. But Schulze knew the apparently peaceful rural scene below was deceptive. Somewhere there, all along their route, there would be watching peasants, signalling their route by flag, radio, bonfire to the next contact until it reached the rebel HQ in the mountains. The rhythmic *thwack*, *thwack*, *thwack* of the rotor blades of the gun-ship overhead was somehow relaxing, but he resisted his inclination to close his eyes and sleep like most of the Headhunters packed in with him in the tight little plane. He wanted to be wide awake and alert if anything happened. You couldn't jump out of a stricken chopper!

Time passed leadenly as the V of helicopters swept over rivers and paddies at 100 kilometres an hour, while the radios crackled back and forth between the formation, giving and receiving information about the enemy units somewhere up ahead that they had been commanded to attack. They started to skirt the mountains. Here and there Schulze could make out the signs of war – a ragged shell-hole, a rusting tank or armoured personnel carrier, a cluster of rough heaps of soil which could have been graves, with here and there a burnt-out, abandoned hut.

Now the radio chatter seemed to intensify and their pilot's pained, pale-faced 'morning-after' look had been replaced by one of alert efficiency. The two gunners, who affected a cowboy hat and wore their .38s strapped low to their hips like Western heroes, started to chew their gum more rapidly. Schulze could almost smell the mounting tension.

He turned in his uncomfortable canvas and leather seat. 'All right, you wet-tails, this is the drill. As soon as we start taking fire from the Slant-eyes, the choppers blast 'em and come down as low as they dare. They're not going to land – even boneheads like you lot know why. We jump, and if any of you barnshitters break a leg or something – hard shit! As soon as we're down, we run like hell for cover. We *don't* mess with the Slant-eyes – is that clear?'

They nodded their helmeted heads.

'I know some of you knuckleheads are too dumb to take a dog out to piss on a post, but our job is to get into that fort and *not* to shoot up a few Viets. Down and out – that's our motto.'

'Lucky Knight . . . Lucky Knight One Zero,' the voice started to crackle over the air waves from the chopper at point.

'Lucky Knight One Zero, we read you Copperhead Two One . . . What's new, buddy?'

'Right on station. Gooks all over the place . . . thousands of them, over.'

The pilot with the bandage around his head grinned painfully. 'Just the thing to cure my goddam headache. All right, Tigers, let's go in and earn our pay this day.'

Rapidly the choppers began to form up into their battle teams of two or three gun-ships flying close together to give each other mutual support, firing their 2.75-inch American rockets on dead reckoning while the two gunners blasted the enemy with their heavy machine-guns. Now they whirled down out of the sky. The jungle loomed up ever larger. Below them, half a dozen small figures broke from the trees and started to run along a dyke between the trees and a paddy field.

'Gooks!' one of the gunners sang out. In the same instant as the pilot banked and began chasing the running figures, he fired. One of the running figures flopped down in the mud. The aircraft commander pulled the trigger of the rocket launcher. The chopper shuddered. Two red rockets zipped towards the running men. *Crash . . . crash . . .* Twin spurts of scarlet. The running men disintegrated and the chopper rocked violently as it flew through the blast.

Now there were Vietnamese everywhere, some running for cover, others standing their ground and firing up at the enemy in the sky. Abruptly there was smoke, noise and falling Viets everywhere as the choppers circled the battlefield, dancing in and out of the smoke at tree-top height to engage the Vietnamese. Rockets hissed down, machine-guns chattered, slugs whined off the metal plates of the choppers.

A rocket hissed in, trailing vicious red sparks after it. It exploded right in the middle of a group of fleeing Viets. They were flung into the suddenly naked trees by the blast and stayed there, limp and lifeless in their branches like some kind of horrible human fruit. A chopper was hit, its rotor blades snapping off one by one before it roared downwards in a vertical dive to smack right into the ground. At once the whole wing went down, spraying the area around it with a tremendous volley of fire. But no one clambered out of the wreckage and ran for cover. 'All fives!' their pilot roared over the intercom. 'No deal!'

As one the wing rose and split up into teams again, dancing in and out of the smoke, orbiting the Vietnamese positions, pouring volley after volley of fire into the men trapped below. Now the whole valley seemed carpeted in their bodies and the volume of fire coming up from their positions was weakening. The pilot of Schulze's plane raised his thumb to Schulze and called into his intercom, 'Hear this . . . hear this, Lucky Knight One Zero, going down . . . follow at one second intervals . . . Dropping Krauts now . . .'

Without warning there was metallic cracking noise above Schulze's head as the helicopters started to descend. His heart seemed to explode in his chest. At once the chopper took a nose-down position. The engines stopped. It began a terrifying free-fall. Objects on the ground loomed up with frightening speed as the chopper dropped in total silence. Animal fear tore at Schulze's guts. This was it! A moment later his fear vanished and was replaced by a burning anger. His bones would smash, his blood would stain the green carpet below, purposelessly. No! He levered himself upwards somehow. 'Stand by!' he cried at his petrified comrades. 'Stand by, you piss-arsed cripples!'

Desperately the pilot fought the stricken plane, his face ashen and drenched with sweat. Suddenly he had it. There was still no noise, but the rotors were moving again. The familiar, wonderful vibrations returned. 'Hang on,' the pilot screamed without turning. 'We're gonna crash!'

Schulze did not understand the words too well, but he knew their meaning. His every muscle tensed. The ground rushed up to meet him. The chopper hit the earth with a great thump. Schulze's head shot forward. An electric shock wave ripped up his legs. But he didn't seem to notice. He was euphoric; they had done it!

'Everybody out!' the two gunners screamed, freeing themselves with frantic fingers from their straps.

The Headhunters needed no urging. They tumbled from the stricken helicopter. Crouched low they doubled away from it as the pilot raised his pistol and fired a green signal flare. A bright orange flash cut the green gloom. A bazooka rocket exploded against the chopper's side. It shook violently. Splinters howled through the air. Schulze ignored them, standing upright and waving his men into the trees as more and more helicopters came in low to drop their human cargoes.

Another rocket came in with a shower of angry sparks and burst in a great spurt of flame. A chopper fell from the sky, twirling round and round like a metal leaf. It hit the ground with a huge thump. Schulze, braving the tracer cutting the air all around him, was nearly thrown off his feet. Choppers danced and pranced at tree top height now. The noise was ear-splitting. Rockets zapped back and forth. Men were dying everywhere. The skeletal, stripped trees were heavy with bits of shattered flesh and rags of uniform. To Schulze's right a clump of palms were beginning to burn. He knew he could wait no longer. He spotted Pansy Petersen, minus his helmet and limping badly. 'Let's get the shit outa here, Lieutenant!' he yelled.

'But the choppers!'

'Let the Amis look after themselves! Come on.' He grabbed hold of the hurt officer. Together they ran awkwardly for the cover of the nearest trees, tracer rippling the elephant grass all around them as the Viets realised they were making a run for it.

'*Di ra. Tien len*!' . . . Move up . . . move up!' the officers rallied their men. They came running out of the cover, a ragged line of screaming men, shooting wildly. The Headhunters went at them like crazy. Bayonets flashed. Shovels slashed. Pistols cracked. Men went down howling with pain on both sides. The Headhunters kept on running. Behind them the line of choppers, trying to cover their stricken comrades, fired a tremendous broadside, like a line of men-o'-war in some eighteenth-century sea battle. The line of Viets simply disappeared, carried away into extinction by that terrible salvo, leaving behind them solely the charred grass and a litter of buckled and twisted rifles.

Five minutes later the surviving Headhunters, with a limping Petersen and a cursing, anxious Schulze in the lead, disappeared into the jungle. They had done it. They were on their way to the besieged fort.

EIGHT

Dawn at Dien Bien Phu.

Colonel Schirmer, his right hand pressed to his bandaged stomach, stared out at the unreal scene, together with the starving, ashen-faced survivors of the night's battle. There were piles of dead, French and Vietnamese, everywhere. But if the defenders starved, the flies feasted. They, too, were everywhere – on the dead, on the wounded, on the faeces and pieces of torn flesh that lay on all sides in that lunar landscape, buzzing lazily like fat black grapes with wings, enjoying the first warmth of the day.

Slowly and painfully Schirmer looked around at the defenders, some of them ready with pistols in their hands not to shoot the enemy but to kill the loathsome grey rats which slunk out of the shadows to eat the wounded and the dead with their bloated bellies from which gas escaped at regular intervals in eerie, frightening obscenity. He wrinkled his nose at the heavy, sickly sweet stench of decaying flesh and wondered just how long these exhausted, starved young men, whose eyes glittered large and fanatical in their emaciated faces, could still go on.

'Casualties coming in!' a harsh, excited voice broke the dawn silence. 'Twelves, twenties and sixes!'

Painfully, helped by White Lightning, Schirmer got to his feet, as the half-tracks began to churn their way through the old dead bringing in their monstrous cargoes. Sweating and gritting his teeth against the burning pain in the pit of his stomach, Schirmer began to assist in unloading the wounded, dying and dead.

Together with White Lightning he pulled down four nude, water-logged bodies. They had massively swollen faces, with eyes bulging like small apples from their features and blue lips three times the normal size. Rigor mortis held their arms up in front of them, with sausage-sized fingers reaching up for the sky. The stench was terrible and flies swarmed in hundreds around the green and red fluid which trickled from their nostrils.

Schirmer wiped the sweat from his streaming brow, while White Lightning watched him anxiously, and staggered over to the next pile just as the first Vietnamese 'hate' of the new day commenced. A mortar bomb socked into the dried mud a few metres away. An orderly went down screaming, his buttocks ripped away, and was propelled by the blast right into the midst of a pile of stinking, bloated corpses. Together they pulled the gasping, frightened medic out and bore him downstairs into the stench of the underground hospital.

They threaded their way through the dead who lay everywhere like abandoned bundles of old rags, staggering every time a shell hit the surface and the lights flickered wildly. All was sweating controlled chaos. The operating theatre was, as usual, packed with casualties. '*Doc, I've got it in the chest . . . Plug up this hole, for God's sake . . . Hurry, Doc, I can't breathe . . . Doc, stay with me, I don't want to die . . . I'm cold as hell, Doc, am I going . . .*'

They laid down their burden and helped to carry over the more seriously wounded to the sweating, cursing surgeons working against time, under the flickering white light until after what seemed an age it was over once more and a weary chief surgeon was saying, 'Twenty for six . . . Not bad, gentlemen – fifty percent saved.'

'For what?' a young doctor asked hollowly.

No one cared to answer that overwhelming question.

Together the two Headhunters crawled into the hole in the side of the corridor which they had made their own. White Lightning unhooked his canteen and with his other hand tendered Schirmer two salt tablets. 'Breakfast,' he announced.

Schirmer smiled wanly and accepted the tablets, which he swilled down with a teaspoonful of precious water. 'Thanks,' he gasped, unable to control the trembling in his legs. 'I've eaten better.'

White Lightning nodded and ate his own 'breakfast'.

Another shell whizzed overhead with the piercing scream of a rushing express train. It exploded with a thunderous roar. The bunker trembled like a live thing. The lights flickered and went out for a moment. The wounded and the madmen set up their usual screaming. The lights went out again and an orderly bellowed, 'Knock that yelling off, will you, or I'll feed you personally to the Slope-heads!'

The screams gave way to low, anxious mumbling and moans.

Schirmer smiled wanly, his hands on his stomach again. 'Obviously the padré at work, Major.'

'Obviously,' White Lightning echoed, his face still anxious as he looked at the man crouching next to him in the hole. 'You've got to take more care of yourself, Skipper. You still ought to be in your cot.'

'Yes, with a big-titted blonde,' Schirmer attempted a joke, but there was no humour in his lack-lustre eyes. 'What did you hear during the night? I'm afraid I couldn't keep the pace up. I had to sleep. My damn guts – '

'Morale still seems good, but some of the men on the second-line units are talking among themselves of surrender.'

'And the Legion?'

'Oh, you know the Legion, Skipper – their officers are telling them there will be no surrender at Dien. They'll go out in a *baroud d'honneur* – the last charge with flags waving and bayonets fixed.'

'Very noble indeed,' Schirmer commented. 'What do *you* think?'

'Privately?'

'Yes.' Schirmer took his eyes off a huge grey rat, the size of a small dog, which was attempting to drag what looked like a severed hand into its hole.

'Surrender. There is no other way out. Air is kaput and I can't see these guys, half-starved, exhausted and short of ammo, not to mention the couple of thousand wounded we've got, attempting to break out through 200 kilometres of rebel-held territory.'

Schirmer sighed. 'Exactly my thoughts. As I've said before,' he said, suddenly very businesslike, 'there will be *no* surrender for us. There can be no surrender. The Slant-eyes will slaughter us anyway. Now what is the situation with weapons?'

'That creep has collected a weapon for every man who can hold one, Skipper.'

'You mean the Schoolmaster?'

'Yes.'

'What else has he found out?'

'Anything about Mercier and the rest of the boys, Skipper?'

'Yes.' The rat had given up attempting to drag the human hand into its too small hole. Instead it crouched there, feasting upon it with quick, savage bites.

'Nothing – not a goddam sausage, except for one curious thing – there's a rumour floating around de Castries's HQ that Mercier has been arrested in connection with some French planters' women and Yank mercenaries who are working with the Frogs – airmen, I think.'

'Mercier . . . women?' Schirmer exclaimed, puzzled. 'That's beyond me.' His voice hardened. 'All right, Major, this is what we'll do. My guess is that the monsoons'll start within the next forty-eight. That will signal one thing.'

'Yeah,' White Lightning looked grim, 'an all-out pre-monsoon attack.'

'Exactly. My guess is that the Slant-eyes will hit us with all they've got some time over the next twenty-four hours.' As if to emphasize his point, a salvo of heavy shells straddled the bunker, sending the wounded and the mad off screaming again. 'Why else all this artillery fire since yesterday?'

'Agreed. Go on Skipper.'

'So this day we've got to get out of here, up to one of those two sally-ports. When they come charging, we're going out.' He licked his cracked, parched lips. 'I don't hold much hope for us, Major,' he said grimly, 'but at least we're going to die like men – on our feet – not like old women on our knees.'

White Lightning nodded his agreement. 'I'm with you, Skipper. Better dead than red, as you say in German.'

'All right, see to it that those who are armed and can walk, even crawl, are to make their way up to the sally-port during the day.'

'I'll see to it, but – '

The bald American never finished his question, for

suddenly there came that bellow again, '*Casualties coming in! . . . Twelves, twenties and sixes!*'

Like two automatons, the Headhunters rose and staggered to the exit, leaving the rat happily gnawing at the hand.

A new day had commenced at Dien Bien Phu.

NINE

It had been a strange night, full of alarms, surprises and sudden frights. To their front the horizon had been lit up a dull purple with the permanent barrage, and although Dien Bien Phu had been some ten kilometres or more away, they had been able to hear the fire-fight clearly enough.

All around they had sensed rather than seen the Slant-eyes, but evidence of their presence was everywhere – dumps, cemeteries, motor pools, hastily erected bamboo lean-tos. Once in the middle of the night they had cautiously skirted a small, dimly-lit camp of such huts and had been surprised by the sound of female laughter and the clink of glasses.

Schulze had taken a chance. Going on alone while the rest crouched tensely in the palms, he had crept to the nearest hut and peered through the slits in the bamboos, coming back to report in an incredulous whisper, 'As I live and breathe, do you know what those Slant-eyes have got over there?'

Pansy Petersen shook his head.

'A shitty knocking-shop! The Slope-heads are going at it like fiddlers' elbows. Lads, we joined the wrong army!'

The Headhunters had laughed hollowly and pressed on, making a wide detour round the rear-line brothel.

At about two that morning they had found further progress barred by a battery of howitzers firing into Dien Bien Phu. Every time they fired the whole area was lit up a glowing red, and even though the sweating, barefoot, Chinese artillerymen were concentrating on their target, they would not help seeing the couple of hundred men trying to slip by.

Petersen and Schulze slipped back into the cover of the tall elephant grass. There weren't enough silenced automatics to go around so the Headhunters set about making their own silencers from sections of hollow bamboo, padded with wet clay and layers of uniform cloth. The task completed, some fifty of them crawled to within twenty metres of the unsuspecting Chinese, outlined a stark black against the red glow.

Petersen had waited until they had all been in position, then his whistle shrilled. As one the Headhunters rose and pressed their triggers. That tremendous, silent volley tore into the unsuspecting Chinese. They went down in their scores, their faces contorted with agony, screaming and attempting to turn in vain. It took only a matter of minutes to finish off the survivors with knife and bayonet. The Headhunters then marched on, leaving a silenced battery behind them.

About three hundred hours they had started to run into the Vietnamese main positions, marked minefields, barbed wire entanglements, shell dumps, the occasional bunker, and everywhere new cemeteries.

'Heaven, arse and cloudburst,' Pansy Petersen had exclaimed, 'are they taking casualties!'

'Couldn't happen to a nicer lot of blokes,' Schulze growled. 'Now, sir, give it another sixty to ninety minutes and it'll be dawn. Where we gonna hide up for the day?'

'Well, it's for sure that we're not going to stay up above ground. I don't think they'll take kindly to a bunch of Round-eyes wandering around *their* battlefield, what?' Petersen replied, as jolly as ever.

Schulze was not in the mood for humour. 'What do you want us to sodding well do then – bury ourselves and look at the taties from below, like these stiffs here?' he snorted sourly.

'Exactly. Now if that isn't a good idea, Schulzi!'

So it had been. They ventured on until they felt it was not safe to go any further and then they had begun to dig their own cemetery, knowing that it would be safe from prying eyes; the Slant-eyes, even the most enlightened of them, had a supersititous dread of graveyards. Then it was dawn and the two hundred men of the Special Para were dug in beneath mounds of new earth, from which protruded broken rifles, surmounted by bullet-holed helmets or straw cartwheel hats to serve as markers. To

the casual observer it was no different from a score
of other Vietnam cemeteries which dotted the battlefield.

Lying flat on their stomachs underneath the earth,
peering through the slits which served as look-outs,
Petersen and Schulze surveyed the besieged fortress as it
emerged and then vanished back into the smoke of
shellfire which shrouded it. Between the bunkers and
their hiding place, the shell-holed, cratered landscape was
littered with bodies, sprawled out in the extravagant
postures of the dead among the churned-up, smoking,
brown earth. There were Algerians and Goums, their
heads shaven save for the pigtail, by which Allah was
supposed to drag them up into a Moslem heaven (though
a cynical Petersen couldn't help thinking that Allah must
have been looking the other way this night, for they still
lay there intermingled with gigantic, black, heathen Sengalese), blond Germans of the Legion, hawk-faced
Moroccans, and everywhere the frail, puny bodies of the
Slant-eyes. Petersen wriggled to make himself a little
more comfortable and took his eyes off a bunch of dead
legionnaires, caught in death in one last feverish gesture
of devotion to duty as they crouched there about to
charge, and whispered to Schulze, 'That's *Huguette*.' He
indicated a long, squat, earth-covered shape covered
partially by drifting gun-smoke, its surface pitted with
steaming shell-holes. 'If they're anywhere, that'll be it.'

Schulze nodded his understanding and followed the
course of the deep trench which ran right round the fort at
a distance of five hundred metres from it. From the way
the red and white angry tracer zipped flatly across the
intervening distance, he could guess it was manned its
whole length. 'That trench is gonna be a sod to get
through, Lieutenant,' he commented grimly.

'I was thinking exactly the same. But if we're gonna
make those sally-ports – you can just see the entrances
over there, and there – we've got to. Somehow,' he
added.

'How?'

'Yes, how? That's the question, as some Tommy scrib-
bler once wrote when you were only a kid tit-sucker.'

Schulze was not amused. He had been in combat long

enough to recognise the signs of a coming push – the
sweating, bent coolies dragging up ammunition crates
under the cover of smoke, the engineers laying their white
tapes through their own minefields, the general hectic
activity to the rear. It wouldn't be long now before the
Slant-eyes attacked in strength and swamped the remaining Frog strongholds with their human wave tactics.
Meanwhile, he – and apparently Pansy, too – hadn't a
clue how to get through their lines and into the fort.

HOW? that was the overwhelming question.

As the sun rose higher and they sweated in their earthen
tombs, Schulze, unable to find a solution to their problem, dozed off despite the rising crescendo of the artillery
fire on both sides. He dreamed that a beautiful nude
woman, with wonderful, enormous breasts, was standing
at the door of her bedroom beckoning him towards an
inviting, luxurious bed, but although he was naked in the
dream himself, save for his helmet and combat boots, he
seemed rooted to the ground. Struggle and curse as he
may, he simply could not move a step forward to take
advantage of her offer.

He awoke, trying to fight off the weight which pressed
down over his mouth. '*W . . . what . . .*' he tried to say,
but the sweaty pressure of Petersen's dirty hand stifled his
question. His mouth pressed so close to Schulze's ear that
the big NCO could inhale the officer's body odour – a
mixture of French perfume and Indo-Chinese sweat.

Petersen whispered cautiously, 'Visitors.' He relaxed
the pressure slowly and Schulze squirmed round to look
through the slit.

A group of some twenty Slant-eyes in black pyjamas,
most of them armed with bazookas and satchel charges,
were filing by behind a line of shuffling, barefoot coolies
carrying picks and shovels, who were disappearing into a
shaft behind the trenchline which neither he nor Petersen
had noticed earlier on as it had been shrouded by smoke.

Curiously Schulze watched their progress until they had
all vanished beneath the earth before saying: 'Now what
do you make of that, Lieutenant? Where do you think
that little lot of slit-ears is off to?'

'Let me ask you a question first, Schulzi?' Petersen replied, suddenly for no apparent reason in a high good mood, his dirty face wreathed in a smile.

'Oh, do let's play little games,' Schulze snorted grumpily. 'What about pat-a-cake, pat-a-cake?'

Petersen ignored the comment. 'Did you notice to what unit the Slant-eyes belonged, Schulzi?'

The big NCO rubbed the sleep out of his red-rimmed eyes. Then he got it. The black bandage around the forehead and the skull-and-crossbones tattoo. 'Yer, those shitting Death Volunteers who hit us at the river that time.'

'Exactly,' Petersen said, obviously very pleased with himself.

'So?'

'So – what, my dear knucklehead, is Uncle Ho's élite outfit doing disappearing down a hole in the ground, which, if my eye doesn't deceive me, seems to be running in the general direction of *Fort Huguette*?'

'And armed with satchel charges and the usual gear for blowing through entrenched positions,' Schulze added excitedly.

'Exactly.'

'The Slant-eyes always use those banana-suckers to lead off an attack – ' He stopped short and stared at Petersen, whose dirty face glowed with barely suppressed excitement.

'That was what I was thinking, Schulzi. Now let us think of it like this. That tunnel, because that is what it is, runs down below the encircling trench we can see above ground.'

Schulze nodded his understanding.

'And it leads to one of those sally-ports. Once the attack starts, those Volunteers blow up the entrance, the rest of the Slant-eyes swarm out from their trench and the battle is won.'

'Yes, but – '

'No, buts, Schulzi. Don't you see how that tunnel could be exactly what we've been looking for?'

'No, Lieutenant.'

'Well, how would it be if instead of Slant-eyes popping out of that hole at the crucial moment like jack-in-the-

box, young handsome Lieutenant Petersen and his merry
men did?'

   'You mean – '

   'I certainly do, my dear knucklehead. Now come, let us
put on our thinking caps and see what we can come up
with . . .'

TEN

Uncle Ho shuffled into the tense, yellow-lit underground bunker, dressed in poorly cut khaki tunic and trousers, a pair of sandals, soled with rubber tyres, on his dirty feet. The assembled officers rose from their desks, but he waved them to be seated in that jocular fashion of his that Giap found objectionably hearty and too obviously proletarian.

'Well, comrades, how are we?' he said amiably.

Giap, the 'Father of the People's Army', frowned. For the last thirty minutes he had been playing his 'great captain' role, the meticulous, sagacious commander who had everything under control; now the old bearded fool came shuffling in like a village headman and spoiled everything. 'Everything is under control, comrade,' he said, repressing his anger.

Uncle Ho beamed at him and stroked his wispy beard. 'Explain to this humble fool what is to happen, Comrade General,' he quavered, playing the part of the old, old man to the hilt.

'We shall attack after dark. On all points of the line. It will be a feint. Our main attack will be on *Huguette*. Once we have dealt with de Castries, the rest of the forts will surrender.'

'And if they don't?'

'We will have the garrison and its commander as our hostages to make them, comrade.'

'Ah, torture, you mean,' Uncle Ho said cheerfully. 'I see. Go on, Comrade General. How will you attack *Huguette*?'

'Comrade Napalm is taking care of that.'

'Good, good, everything running smoothly then, I see.' Uncle Ho waved a cheery hand at them. 'Well, I'll be on my way.' He shuffled towards the door in his oversized, rubber-soled sandals, then stopped, as if he had suddenly had a thought. 'Our friends from up north' – Ho meant the 'advisers' from the Chinese Red Army Military Mission – 'maintain it would be better for Dien Bien Phu to fall before the monsoon really sets in. Otherwise, they feel they might not be in a position to keep up supplies down the highway. Victory, comrades.' He ambled out.

'Victory, comrade,' Giap echoed hollowly. He had taken the hint. Perhaps the Chinese 'advisers' *had* made a remark of that kind, or perhaps it came from Ho himself – he knew just how much Ho was opposed to this open confrontation with the French, instead of the old evasive guerilla tactics. But wherever it had come, it meant one thing: if Dien Bien Phu did not fall in the next forty-eight hours, they – Ho and the Chinese – would call off the offensive. The casualties the regulars had suffered had been too heavy. They would sack him and revert to the old strategy. Realising for the very first time how lonely a great commander was and knowing instinctively that his staff was withdrawing from him (they had read Ho's meaning correctly, too), Giap stared grimly at the barometer which was falling rapidly. The rains would be on him soon.

General de Castries smiled winningly at his staff officers as the command bunker shook under the shellfire, with the grey cement dust coming down in a fine rain from the roof. But the more perceptive among his officers, mostly those of the Legion, could see the elegant ex-cavalry officer's inner tension. His days of confident boasting were over and his visits to the crowded underground hospital with the shoulder-pat here and word of cheer there were infrequent, very infrequent; there were too many casualties and they reminded him of what desperate straits the garrison was in.

'Gentlemen,' he commenced the evening briefing, 'I will be frank with you . . . brutally frank.'

The Legion officers looked at each other and winked. They knew that 'frank' meant lies and 'brutally frank' meant even bigger ones.

'At the moment we are locked up deep in Viet Minh-controlled territory and there is no way of our getting out.

I have already dismissed the possibility of a successful break-out and withdrawal. Alternatively there is little chance of a land force fighting its way through to reprieve the garrison. In essence, gentlemen, we are faced with a stalemate, not with the disaster that some of you, I've heard, are forecasting for Dien Bien Phu.' He looked pointedly at the Legion officers, who grouped together. The representatives of the seven Legion para battalions which made up the garrison's élite troops stared back at him woodenly. De Castries flushed and continued. 'Time is on our side. All we need to do is to stick it out – ' his words were drowned by the explosion of a 155mm shell only metres away. De Castries blanched but caught himself in time – 'stick it out, as I was saying, until the monsoons come. Then, gentlemen, I confidently predict our good friend, General Giap, will quietly disappear into the trees from which, to judge from his rather ape-like appearance, his ancestors came not so long ago, what.'

His sally was greeted by polite laughter from his toadies, but the Legion officers remained stonily silent. They did not underestimate the one-time grammar-school teacher of history, who had had the good fortune *not* to attend St Cyr; their casualties were too high for that.

De Castries frowned and raised his voice above the chatter of machine-guns close by. 'Gentlemen, I say this to you on this first day of May, give me rain and I'll give you stalemate, at the worst – and at the best, *victory*!' He flung an involuntary glance at his weather officer, a bespectacled, weedy graduate from the Sorbonne. But the met man looked down at his boots stubbornly, almost as if he were ashamed for not having produced the much needed monsoon. The barrage went on.

'Dismiss!' de Casties snapped in sudden anger. They dismissed.

The ancient coolie waved his hissing carbide lamp and guided his tall, gaunt visitor down the shaft, while awed, frightened workers pressed to one side to make way for him. Ahead of them the old man's lamp threw monstrous shadows on the earthen walls of the shaft and the darkness was full of the eerie scampering of many clawed feet.

'Rats,' the old man chuckled hoarsely. 'As big as pigs they are. There's plenty of human meat up there for them to feed on, eh.' He pointed a trembling dirty forefinger upwards at the battlefield.

Napalm didn't comment. They were probably just below the French line now. Perhaps the enemy had buried sensors underneath the surface to check for saps like this; talking too much or too loudly might give them away.

They plodded on along the lines of duckboards, with here and there a young sentry, masked against the underground gases, springing to attention as Napalm passed, his eyes above the cotton bulging with fear when they saw who was passing.

A light approached them, accompanied by a weird, low moan. The guide turned to Napalm and grinned, revealing a single, crooked tooth. 'Don't worry,' he cackled and tapped his temple with a gnarled shaking finger. 'One of those coolies who's gone off his head. Cracked as a pisspot. Lot of them go like that down here.' A moment later a coolie staggered by them, his eyes vacant and mad and a strange, eerie, meaningless dirge coming from his parched lips. 'Cracked as a pisspot,' the guide quavered as the mad coolie disappeared.

Now it started to get lighter and Napalm could hear the busy scrape of many shovels. They swung round a sharp bend – set thus to prevent any explosive blast sweeping straight down the tunnel – and stopped.

Ahead of them at the rock face, naked coolies, their only clothing knee-pads, were hacking and clawing at the dark surface, while others shovelled the loose earth and rocks onto little trolleys and sledges, which waiting coolies, the straps already fastened around their foreheads, were ready to draw to the surface.

The under-lieutenant in charge saw Napalm and snapped to attention. 'Victory, Comrade Captain,' he rasped.

'Victory, comrade,' Napalm replied routinely. 'Well?'

'Another two metres – three at the most – and we're through.' He pointed to the glistening pool of water at his feet and then at the steady drip-drip of moisture just above his head. 'That's coming down from the surface, comrade. So we can tell we're close.'

'I see.' Napalm viewed the efforts of his sweating, gasping coolies for a moment, telling himself that at least two of them wouldn't survive the night. But then that was the price of victory that they must all pay, including the two hundred of his original thousand who had died of rockfalls, suffocation and exhaustion. 'What is your prediction?' he snapped.

The officer looked at his glowing green compass. 'If the compass is accurate, then we're accurate, too, Comrade Captain. Give or take a metre, we should be just outside the northern sally-port.'

'I see.'

'Of course, if it starts pissing down upstairs . . .'

Napalm frowned at the coarseness, but the under-lieutenant could not see the frown and continued.

'. . . then we're really in trouble. It'll come through, especially when the monsoon really gets going.'

'We will be up and into the fort by the time the monsoon starts, comrade,' Napalm said severely.

The other man wasn't convinced. 'It's very stuffy down here, comrade,' he said. 'That's always a sign the monsoon's upon us.'

Napalm ignored the comment. 'Now these are your orders, Comrade Lieutenant. One, you will continue digging upwards, resting just below the surface three hours before dawn. Two, from now onwards there will be absolute silence; no smoking, no coughing – nothing that might attract the enemy's attention. We are too close to the surface now. Three, my Volunteers will begin entering the tunnel at three hours before dawn, not a moment before. I can't risk this foul air affecting them. Four, as soon as you receive the word from the surface, start pulling out the remaining coolies. Clear?'

'Clear, Comrade Captain. But I still maintain we'll have the rains before then.'

Captain Napalm turned without a word. The man was a fool. Pity the engineer-lieutenant wasn't in the Volunteers. He would have him lead the first wave – and perish.

White Lightning mopped his dripping brow and lifted his head towards the air-hole in the side of the sally-port. He breathed in deeply, but the air which came was as wet and hot as that within *Fort Huguette*. 'Phew,' he sighed to Schirmer. 'It's like a goddam Turkish bath in here!'

Schirmer nodded, his breath coming in short, painful gasps. Like everyone else in the tight chamber, Headhunters and members of the Legion para battalion alike, he was short of breath, his face was lathered in sweat and his shirt was black with the stuff. In all his time in Indo-China he had never known it to be so hot. The monsoon *must* break soon.

'What do you think, sir?' Tod asked. The little torturer, who had suffered slight burns during the ambush on Route 41 was in better shape than the rest, but he, too, was gasping as if he were going to suffer a heart attack at any moment. 'Do you think they'll come before the rains do?' The fear was undisguised in the dark eyes behind the thick-lensed glasses.

'I should think so,' Schirmer said easily and wiped the sweat off the rifle that Tod had taken from one of the dead for him. 'I doubt if General Giap will do us the favour of letting us get out of this mess without a fight.'

'But there is a latrine rumour going round that General de Castries thinks the rains will come first.'

'Latrine rumours, Schoolmaster,' Schirmer said wearily, 'deserve to end where they start – *in the shit!*' He looked across at the bald American. 'What time do you make it?'

'Nearly twelve, sir.'

'Midnight. Another four and a half hours till dawn.' Schirmer wiped his face free of sweat for the umpteenth time and stared around at his Headhunters, who looked as worn and as pale as he did. They were all armed and determined, but what could they do against the Slanty-eyed hordes, he asked himself. For a few moments he toyed with the idea of ordering the NCO in charge of the massive steel door of the sally-port to open it. His men were past-masters of clandestine warfare; they would be better on their own out in the darkness. But only for a moment. His good sense told him that the weeks in the underground hospital on poor food had weakened them too much; they would never stand the pace.

White Lightning seemed to sense what was going

through his CO's head, for he raised his thumb in the American sense of confidence and hope and whispered across, 'Never fear, Skipper, we'll beat the crappy Slopeheads yet.'

Schirmer smiled wearily. 'Yes, we'll beat them, Major.' But there was no hope in his voice.

ELEVEN

It was beginning to drizzle now, a faint, soft, warm rain, but the wind was rising and black clouds were scudding across the night sky. Every now and again the shell-stripped trees shivered violently and abandoned capes flapped alarmingly; the monsoon was not far off.

Like grey ghosts the Headhunters stole from their graves. The lack of sound, save for the drip-drip of the rain, was uncanny and somehow unsettling after the heavy bombardment of the day. In single file – every man tense, alert, ready – they worked their way through the rear lines of the enemy. To their front a wet mist hung over the battlefield like a cloak. But its damp clinging greyness could not quite conceal the faint noises that came from it. The soft clink of equipment, the scrape of a nailed boot, the stifled cough. There were men out there – many of them – awake and alert. Why? Schulze asked himself. Was it this night when the Slant-eyes would launch their final, all-out offensive on the besieged garrison? He dismissed the problem and concentrated on the task at hand as they crept ever nearer to the entrance to the shaft.

They stumbled into an ammunition pit filled with half-awake coolies and slit their throats before the coolies were aware of what was happening to them. A sentry loomed up suddenly from nowhere. He was clubbed and slaughtered as he was trying to unsling his rifle and sound the alarm. A flare hissed alarmingly into the air, bathing the Headhunters, frozen into immobility, in its icy silver light. Schulze hardly dared breathe. Somebody *must* spot them. The burst of machine-gun fire which would slaughter them *must* come at any moment. Yet nothing happened. There was no sound save the soft drip-drip of the rain. Finally, the flare dropped to the ground and he breathed a sigh of relief, suddenly blinded by the darkness. They crept on.

They were perhaps a hundred metres from the entrance to the tunnel, wending their way cautiously on tip-toe between the piles of ammunition cases and supplies which littered the area when the whispered command to halt came down the column. They waited there, tense and worried, their hearts pounding while the scouts dealt with whatever had stopped them. The signal for them to move forward came again. In single file they passed two sentries: the one with a combat knife protruding from between his shoulder blades; the other, his face a contorted crimson and his tongue hanging out like a piece of liver, with the chicken wire with which the scout had strangled him imbedded deep in the flesh of his skinny yellow neck.

'Amen!' Schulze whispered in mock piety as he filed by and tipped his kepi.

'*Wire . . . trip wires!*' a voice whispered urgently.

Schulze nodded to Petersen. Together they crept past the rest to where the scout was kneeling in the wet grass. A thin wire had been looped cunningly through the shattered stumps of trees which barred the entrance to the shaft.

'Tried to pull it up,' the scout explained in a whisper. 'Too tough for me.'

'Yer, too much of the right-handed widow,' Schulze grunted scornfully. 'Saps yer strength, yer know . . . Lieutenant, you check –'

Petersen was gone before he could finish the request, checking the length of wire to right and left for cans filled with pebbles, bells or empty shell-cases, or any other of the devices the Viets used to sound the alarm. There were none.

Schulze nodded his understanding. He bent his massive shoulders, seized the wire in both paws and heaved. It parted at once with a brittle snap. Schulze froze. The noise had seemed tremendous. Surely it must have alerted the sentries somewhere in the entrance to the tunnel. But nothing happened. Schulze sighed. 'Great crap on the Christmas tree, Lieutenant,' he whispered to Petersen, 'somebody up there must like us. We can't be that damned lucky!'

'Let's hope we go on being lucky, you big rogue,'

Petersen whispered. 'Now let's see about nobbling those sentries in there. Move it!'

Schulze and Petersen advanced on the entrance, from which a faint chink of light came and the soft muted sounds of tired, middle-of-the-night voices. They halted outside the sacking which obscured the entrance to the shaft. Schulze's nostrils were assailed by the stink of rotten fish-paste at close hand. The sentries were just behind the sacking! He pulled his combat knife from his boot and signalled to Petersen to take up his position. The officer nodded his understanding and, pulling out his knife, grasped the edge of the curtain with his free hand.

Schulze waited until he had done that, then nodded again and hissed 'Three'.

Noiselessly, the two tense men, their every nerve tingling electrically, counted to three.

'*Now!*' Schulze hissed.

Petersen pulled aside the sacking. Three Volunteers sat on the other side, on looted chairs, one eating from a bowl of rice with his chopsticks poised between mouth and bowl ludicrously as his mouth gaped in surprise. Schulze's knife flashed. The Volunteer's cry of alarm ended in a thick gurgle of blood. His eyes rolled upwards and he sank to the floor, his chopsticks still clutched in a hand, already dead. Schulze sprang over his body and grabbed the next nearest Volunteer, pulling him off his feet, his eyes bulging from fear and legs kicking. Schulze drew back his hamlike fist and smashed it cruelly into the Viet's face. The face shot back, a ruined mess, with the neck broken. For a moment Schulze held him there like a broken doll, while behind them Petersen stabbed the third Viet to death, then dropped him to the floor. The entrance to the tunnel was theirs!

Schulze wiped the blood off his knuckles on the dead man's uniform and then gave the hand signal the anxious men outside had been waiting for. Hurriedly they filed inside and Petersen started making his dispositions. He posted a platoon at the entrance to the tunnel and directed them to set up a light machine-gun there, while the two scouts remained outside to scatter deballockers to the right and left of the opening and give advance notice of anyone approaching. Finally he was ready to move on.

'And remember,' he warned the little machine-gun team, 'everything depends upon you men holding this exit if the balloon goes up.'

'We won't let you down, sir,' the men chanted in unison.

'You'd better not,' Schulze added his own warning in a low growl, 'or Uncle Schulze will work you over.' He blew on his battered knuckles. 'You'll be lacking a set of ears before you know.' The Headhunters started to file deeper into the tunnel.

They moved swiftly, but cautiously down the winding, ill-lit passage where the only sounds came from the scurrying of the rats that were everywhere, the soft shuffle of their sock-covered feet and the steady drip-drip of the moisture which penetrated from the earthen ceiling above. Petersen and Schulze in the lead had their grease-guns at the ready while they advanced, their bodies slightly bent as if they were fighting a strong wind.

Schulze was not usually a sensitive man, but there was something unholy – eerie – about the tunnel which made the small blond hairs at the back of his bull-neck stiffen. Why, he didn't really know. He expected something very frightening to appear around the very next bend, but nothing did.

Once his heart leapt into his mouth when a gigantic shadow suddenly appeared on the wall ahead, flickering slightly in the glaring yellow light of the carbide lamp that hung on a wooden beam to his right. He caught himself from crying out just in time. Next instant the shadow disappeared in a soft patter of clawed feet.

'A rat,' Petersen commented, with only a slight tremor in his voice.

'Jesus wept,' Schulze cursed. 'I've just gone and pissed in me knickers, Lieutenant!'

Petersen hadn't the strength to laugh.

They went on.

Petersen's hopes started to rise. They must have progressed half the length of the tunnel, he estimated. Perhaps another five – maybe ten – minutes and they would be at the end of the tunnel. What he would find there, Petersen did not exactly know. He guessed, however, that the diggers, whoever they were, would not have broken through to the surface yet, but they'd be damn close. With a bit of luck, the Headhunters would be able to break through quickly and rush across the intervening ground to the sally-port under cover of the rain. Once there, they would have to get Colonel Schirmer and his party out and back into the tunnel while the darkness still held. He realised suddenly just how risky and full of imponderables their plan was, but there was no other way.

'Sir,' Schulze caught hold of his arm and restrained him from moving. 'Hark at that!' He cocked his head to one side, a finger held to his lips.

Petersen did the same. For a moment he could make out nothing. Then he heard it. The sound of shovels and picks scraping at the earth. They were near the exit. He swallowed hard and by means of hand signals indicated to the men crouched behind him to be extra careful. As if they were walking across eggs, they continued, placing each foot down deliberately, picking their way round the ever increasing pools of water which might have betrayed their presence. The sound of working got closer and closer.

They swung round a bend and almost walked straight into the guard, turned inwards with his back to the naked coolies sweating at the rock-face. His mouth opened with shock. Almost instinctively he pressed the trigger of his grease-gun. Slugs howled all around the Headhunters. Two men were bowled over, screaming with agony. The remainder surged forward with a wild yell. At the rock face the coolies turned, their sweat-lathered yellow faces contorted with fear, rage and hate. As the Headhunters swamped the guard, trampling him under their running feet, the diggers charged, swinging their picks and shovels. The two groups clashed in the centre of the passage.

Schulze, caught off guard, slipped and went down in the mud, with a stinking coolie writhing on top of him and trying to smash in his head with a pick-handle. Somehow Schulze managed to turn in the mire; he thrust his big foot in the man's naked middle and with a grunt and heave sent him flying through the air. The next instant he was on his feet, slipping through the mud, angrily stamping his boot

into the prostrate coolie's face, as if he were stamping out
a fire, until finally it was a bloody, gory mess and he
stopped.

By then the little clash was over. There were unconscious, bloody coolies and the occasional Headhunter
pressed into the churned-up mire of the floor.

Petersen wiped a cut scalp and commanded, 'All right,
don't stand around like a lot of wet dreams – get those
shovels and picks! Time's a-passing. At that face!'

They needed no urging. While some of them cleared
away the coolies, smashing in the skulls of those still alive
with the sledgehammers for good measure, the remainder
seized the abandoned tools and set to, clearing away the
remaining earth and rocks. Almost at once cooler air
started to infiltrate into the tunnel and the carbide lamps
began to flicker. Petersen knew they weren't far off. An
almost overwhelming excitement overcame him. They
were going to do it! He grabbed a shovel himself and
found himself working at Schulze's side, attempting to
tear out a huge rock which barred further progress at their
end of the face.

The minutes passed in hectic activity. The first large
flurry of soil revealed the dark patch of sky. They redoubled their efforts. The hole grew larger. Rain started
to come in, wetting their upturned, happy faces. They
gave a subdued cheer. They were almost done now. Suddenly a Headhunter was scrambling through the hole,
poking his head through to survey the area around the
exit. He reported a moment later, 'Can't see anything, sir.
Shall we have a go?'

Swiftly, Petersen picked the small team that would go
with him – Schulze and six Headhunters, all festooned
with grenades and armed with silenced grease-guns. 'The
rest of you,' he ordered, 'hang on here and keep alert.
Hopefully we shouldn't be long.'

'Good luck, sir,' someone said emotionally as Petersen
started to clamber through the hole, 'and you, too,
Sergeant-Major Schulze.'

'Oh, kiss me quick, I think I'm gonna have a period,'
Schulze snorted scornfully. 'Get off it, you soft shit!' And
with that he was gone as well.

Crouched low, the rain beating down more heavily

now and flares sailing into the night sky further to the
north with ever increasing frequency, they doubled towards the squat hulk of *Fort Huguette*. Somewhere in the
gloom, a voice called something in a language they
couldn't understand.

'Keep going!' Petersen ordered.

The voice called again. It was too much for Schulze.
'Shitting Slope-head!' he growled and tossed a grenade in
the direction from which the challenge had come. A thick
muffled crump, a flash of purple flame and an agonizing
scream. For a moment there was a heavy, echoing silence.
Then tracer started to curve towards them, glowing alternatively white and red and gaining in speed the closer it
got. A Headhunter went down in the mud without a
sound. Another bent to help, but Schulze kicked him hard
as he doubled by, crying, 'Keep moving . . . keep moving,
can't you see the poor shit's bought it?'

Two men ran towards them. Petersen recognised them
as Slant-eyes immediately by their conical straw hats. He
pressed the trigger of his grease-gun. It trembled almost
noiselessly at his hip. They went down, writhing in the
mire. They sprang over a wire-fence. Cans filled with
pebbles started to jingle at once. A machine-gun chattered. A Headhunter screamed and dropped his grease-
gun, his right arm suddenly paralysed. 'I'm all right,' he
called, 'keep on going!'

'What do you think we were going to do, you silly
prick,' Schulze snorted, 'sit down here and have a shitting
picnic?' He pushed the wounded man ahead of him and,
turning, sprayed the area from which the machine-gun
fire was coming. It stopped at once. They ran on. Now
they were almost up to the sally-port and Petersen could
see the great metal door that closed it. Now, he told
himself, his chest heaving with the effort of running, they
could really be in trouble, while they convinced the defenders that they were friendly and they should open it.
Still running, he fumbled with the smoke grenade at his
belt. He freed it, and then the phosphorus grenade which
was clipped on next to it. 'Down!' he gasped when they
were a matter of metres from the door. 'Down
everywhere!'

The next instant he flung the smoke grenade. It exploded with a soft crump and started emitting thick white smoke at once. Beyond it the phosphorus grenade exploded immediately afterwards and started to burn blindingly. At once the enemy machine-guns concentrated on the flames, just as Petersen had hoped they would. Protected by the smoke, he doubled towards the steel door, followed by the rest. His butt crashed against it hollowly. 'We're French,' he cried. 'French, for Chrissake – let us in before the Slant-eyes spot us!'

Nothing happened. The machine-gun slugs started to swing in their direction. Petersen slammed the butt of his grease-gun at the door again. 'You pricks! Crazy, deaf, yellow Frog pricks!' he screamed, desperately trying to remember the French cusswords, as the tracer drew ever nearer, '*LET US IN . . . LET US IN*!'

And then when Petersen was already beginning to cringe, knowing that he would be ripped apart by machine-gun fire at any moment, the door started to swing open and Schulze was crying joyously at the top of his voice as he stumbled forward, eyes blinking in the sudden light, towards an astounded Colonel Schirmer, 'Make way for the shit-shovellers . . . make way.' Trampling over the outstretched feet and thrusting aside the men in his way, he seized Schirmer in a huge bear-hug, swinging the Colonel off his feet. Tears of joy running down his red, honest face. They had done it; *they had got into Fort Huguette*!

TWELVE

Violently the lightning ripped the night sky apart. The rain poured down and the battlefield was flooded with a blood-red light. The men emerging from the fort crouched as one. Before them the battlefield was revealed in all its stark, sombre glory: the trees, stripped of their foliage, looking like gaunt, outsize toothpicks; the mutilated carcasses of shot-up tanks and trucks and crashed planes; and everywhere discarded equipment, rifles, gas-masks, empty cans, bits and pieces of uniform. But it wasn't the sobering tableau of the battlefield which caught the crouching men's attention: it was the long lines of black figures crossing the littered, shell-holed ground, rifles held at the high port across their skinny chests. Thousands of them. It was the last human wave attack. Then the light died and the battlefield was virtually invisible again.

Petersen and Schulze rose instantly. 'Come on,' they urged. 'We've not much time.'

The men behind them needed no urging. Hurriedly they started splashing and wading through the thigh-deep puddles, soaked uniforms sticking to their emaciated bodies, heading for the entrance to the tunnel where already helping hands were reaching up to aid them inside.

Suddenly they stopped again. There was a sound unlike anything they had heard for many a year. It started in the distance, a dull, groaning noise which most of them had last heard on the snowbound steppes of Russia. Six separate times it sounded. The horizon was lit by the bright scarlet flashes. For a moment the scared fugitives were mesmerized, then Schulze shouted, '*Stalin organs – they're using Stalin organs!*' just as, with a baleful scream of elemental fury, the multiple rockets howled above their heads to slam into *Huguette*. They ran frantically for the cover of the hole, all attempts at concealment cast aside now.

Captain Napalm, surveying the area of the sally-port with his night glasses just before he led his Volunteers into the tunnel, knew instantly what had happened. The tall, terribly disfigured Vietnamese with the mask wasted no time in recriminations, questions, hesitancies. He gave his orders at once. 'Bugler – sound the charge!' he hissed.

The boy looked up at him, his gaunt figure outlined a glowing red against the background of the barrage, in bewilderment. 'Charge – but where?'

'The entrance to the tunnel!'

The boy put the bugle to his lips and blew with all his strength. Napalm thrust forward an outstretched hand to indicate the direction. With a cheer his men charged forward, bayonets at the ready. They ran into the deballockers and went down on all sides howling with agony, grabbing feverishly at their ruined crotches and writhing back and forth in the mud as they died a terrible death. Napalm bore a charmed life. The deadly little mines exploded on all sides as his men put their feet on them, but he escaped unhurt.

The French machine-guns began to chatter. Tracer curved in the direction of the running men. A soldier threw a grenade. It missed. Next instant he went down, almost cut in half. Another grenade sailed through the air and exploded just in front of the machine-gun. It blinded the gunner for an instant. That instant sufficed. A Volunteer, his body wrapped in explosive charges for the assault on the sally-port, ran straight into the gun, taking a whole belt of tracer. Next moment he disintegrated in a great, earth-shaking explosion, taking the gun and its crew with him.

The survivors doubled forward, while behind them the battlefield shook with the impact of the bombardment, and a great roar rose from the throats of thousands of men as the human wave rolled forward to be churned and broken into a mess of red, bloody gore by the scores of French shells which descended upon it. But already it was being succeeded by the next wave.

Napalm flung himself down next to the body of a dead Frenchman half-buried in the thick mud and surveyed the scene, knowing that the enemy must be cleared out of the tunnel if he and his Volunteers were to die for the cause in the most fitting way. On the battlefield the third wave went in, rolling up and over the hundreds of dead bodies which already lay to their front. Napalm rose to his feet. If they didn't reach the sally-port in time, all that sacrifice would be in vain.

'Death Volunteers,' he cried in a thin reedy voice, '*follow me!*' He thrust aside the blinded bugler, who was groping his way forward, two scarlet pits where his eyes had been, hand outstretched. The boy fell on his face into the mud and drowned, as the boots of the eager Volunteers pushed him deeper and deeper into the puddle.

They pelted into the tunnel, pushing and clawing at each other in their eagerness to die. Three and four abreast, their skinny chests heaving with the effort, their dark slant-eyes glittering fanatically with the usual drugs, they raced down the passageway. Up ahead, there was the sound of other boots running to meet them. Headhunters and Volunteers were set on a collision course.

The leading Headhunters swung round the bend and skidded to a stop. The Volunteers fired and did the same. There was a confused, wild exchange of shots and then both sides were drawing back to cover hastily, leaving their dead behind them.

Schirmer flopped to the ground, as a burst of shots ripped along the earth just where he had been standing a moment before, and gasped, 'What in three devils' name was that . . . that monstrosity in a mask?'

'I don't know, sir,' Schulze gasped. 'All I know is that if we don't get out of here soon, we're knackered.' As if to emphasize his point, earth and pebbles came cascading down from the ceiling as another salvo of French shells fell on the battlefield above them. 'It's max effort for them, and the Slant-eyes have got to get through this tunnel, come what may!'

'I know . . . I know,' Schirmer cried, holding his stomach, realising for the first time just how weak he was; the exertion was simply too much for him. 'But what – '

The grenade came tumbling down the incline round the bend. 'Duck!' someone screamed, drowning Schirmer's words. A young Headhunter dived forward and flung himself on to it just as it exploded. His body heaved, then burst apart, hosing those crouched fearfully against the wall opposite in hot blood. What was left of the smoking body sagged onto the charred floor.

'*I can't see . . . can't see*!' another Headhunter moaned, and before anyone could stop him he had staggered directly into the enemy fire. He crumpled and lay there twitching violently as slug after slug smacked into his dying body; then he was still.

'My God, they're slaughtering us!' White Lightning cried as yet another grenade exploded just short of them, sending red-hot slivers of razor-sharp steel howling through the air.

A Headhunter crashed to the floor, blood jetting scarlet from a severed leg. Schulze crawled over to him and started making a tourniquet, his fingers wet and sticky with the man's blood, while Petersen jammed his whole clenched fist into the great hole in order to stem the flow.

Wildly Schirmer cast around for some way to escape from this murderous trap. Suddenly he spotted it a little to their rear: a pile of jerricans, neatly stacked up nearly to the roof. Ignoring the burning ache in the pit of his stomach, he limped back to them and swung down the topmost can. It was heavy – and full. '*Gott sei dank*!' he breathed and swung down to face up the corridor, just in time to see one of his men neatly boot a grenade back the way it had come but failed to note its companion that had landed between his legs. It was a fatal oversight. Next moment it had exploded. Suddenly the Headhunter was a screaming dwarf, hobbling along on shattered thighs, leaving a bloody trail behind him before he finally keeled over and died.

'The last twelve men – up here at the double!' Schirmer commanded, his breath coming in short, painful gasps. 'Quick – empty your canteens of water!'

While they did so, he tugged open the jerry can and waited to pour its contents. 'First man, you, hold out your canteen.' The man did so, puzzled. Hastily Schirmer filled it to the brim, spilling the gas in his haste. 'Now the next man . . . and the next.' Rapidly, he filled canteen after canteen, his trembling hands stinking of spilled fuel. Finished he cried, 'Come on, follow me!'

They doubled back to where the others were crouched. 'All right, you men, get a handkerchief or any piece of cloth – rip up your shirts, if you have to, but get some cloth. You with the canteens, too.'

Bewildered but obedient, they did as they were told.

'Right, all of you, piss on the cloth and wrap it around your face. We're going in as soon as these beauties explode.'

Frantically the Headhunters ripped open their flies and carried out their anxious CO's order.

'But I can't seem to do it,' Tod quavered fearfully. 'I've got no urine left!'

'Here, have some of mine – genuine gnat's piss!' Schulze sprayed a great yellow stream across the Schoolmaster's trembling hands and the cloth they held.

Schirmer waited no longer. The barrage over them was making the whole tunnel shake and tremble. Earth poured down upon them, and acrid cordite fumes were beginning to drift in from the other end. Time was running out fast. 'You men with the canteens, prepare to throw!' He took the thermite grenade from his webbing pelt and pulled the pin. 'Are you ready? *THROW*!'

Man after man grunted and heaved his makeshift grenade around the bend. One got a bullet through his shoulder. He staggered under the impact and went down on his knees, his face contorted with agony, but somehow he managed to throw his canteen all the same.

Schirmer didn't hesitate. He sprang round the bend. The tunnel was packed with Slant-eyes. They yelled with rage, their pyjamas dripping with gas, but reacted just a moment too late. Schirmer hurled his grenade and ducked as the slugs cut the air where his upper body had been.

The tunnel ahead exploded in a sheet of blue, searing flame. In an instant the Volunteers there were writhing living torches, engulfed in flames.

Captain Napalm gasped with horror. His one withered arm rose to protect his mutilated face, trying to ward off that terrible ball of flame that was hurtling towards him. '*NO*!' he screamed hysterically as it ignited on his chest with a tremendous searing pain. He went down on his knees, wreathed in the burning fury, trying to fight it off with hands that were getting weaker by the instant. It tore at his mask, that vanished in a flash of scorched silk to reveal that monstrous face. His nostrils were full of the stench of burning flesh. Strangled, inhuman, animal cries were coming from his heat-scorched lungs. His flesh started to bubble under the tremendous heat and he was down on the floor, that terrible face lying in a pool of burning-blue gasoline that ate it away forever.

'Get going!' Schirmer smacked White Lightning on the back and propelled him forward. He stumbled on, half-blinded by the burning smoke, his feet crunching over burning charred bodies, his nostrils assailed by the awful stink of cooked flesh. Man after man followed him, falling and tripping over the corpses, already burnt into rigid poses with blackened claws, through which the bones showed through a gleaming white, extended upwards, as if intent on tripping them. How he managed that horrible corridor of death, Schirmer never knew later; its horror seemed never-ending. But suddenly, somehow or other, he was outside in the glittering, open air, with the immense barrage transforming the night into day and tiny barefoot figures already visible on the roof of *Fort Huguette*, glimpsed through the fog of war, as they hauled up their black flag of victory at Dien Bien Phu. Then he, like the rest, was running for life to the jungle beyond.

Dien Bien Phu had fallen. The French colonial empire in Indo-China was finished.

Epilogue

Colonel Mercier, standing on the dais to the rear of the notables, smiled bitterly. At last the rats were emerging from their gold-plated bunkers to welcome the new masters. French and Viets, they had lost an empire and now they were nodding and smiling and stroking their well-fed paunches as they parleyed with the crew-cut, bewildered new boys, as if they had achieved something. What did a century of sweat and blood mean to these opportunists, for whom money and prestige came first? Did they ever think, at that terrible three o'clock of a sleepless morning, about the thousands of young men, some hardly more than children and of many nationalities, who had died so terribly these last eight years to fill their purses, line their paunches, cover their immaculately-uniformed chests with decorations? Could they realise that they had – directly – ruined France, reducing his beloved country to little better than a fourth-class power, an adjunct of another power some five thousand kilometres away across a great ocean? Of course, they couldn't. Despite their wealth, their prestige, their titles, they were little men in spirit: the men of 1940 still who had ruined France. Was there any hope for a country governed by men like that?

He dismissed them as unworthy of his consideration and took in the Saigon scene with his shrewd little eyes: the military police from the Legion who were everywhere; the barricaded, sandbagged shops and official buildings; the streams of long luxurious cars and trucks, bearing the possessions of the new masters of Indo-China. '*Coca-Cola and the greenback economy*,' he whispered to himself cynically. Not quite the tools to win the new war that would be waged here soon.

Down at the docks the sirens of the troopship began to

shrill. As if in answer the Legion band struck up the *Boudin*. Round the corner of the great, tree-lined avenue, the survivors of the lost battle for Indo-China faces set under their immaculate white kepis, swung, marched in that slow deliberate gait of the Legion. 'The First Parachute Battalion of the Legion,' the new commanding general in Saigon, who had replaced the disgraced General Navarre, announced.

'A battalion,' the crew-cut general in civilian clothes breathed.

'Je-zus, it's no bigger than one of our companies!'

'The Second Parachute Battalion!'

Mercier, his one arm raised in the salute, watched the survivors march by with tears in his eyes. Twelve thousand of them had died in battle, including virtually every commanding officer – and for nothing. Now they were returning to Africa to fight another dirty war for a country that didn't want or deserve them. The tears started to flow down his cheeks.

Colonel Schirmer, followed by White Lightning hobbling along with the aid of a stick, came round the corner at that slow majestic pace of the Legion. Behind him the Headhunters – what was left of them – marched with set looks on their bronzed, emaciated faces, their eyes hard and bitter.

'*Special Battalion* – eyes right!' he commanded and swung up his right hand in slow deliberation, his gaze piercing the new boys with their soft, bewildered, well-fed faces. They had the machines and unlimited supplies of money, but they would fail, too; he knew it instinctively.

Behind him Sergeant-Major Schulze, a look of contempt on his scarred face as he viewed the watching Amis on the dais, barked, '*Headhunters – a song*!'

The wingman, his right arm gone, amputated with a jungle knife and without anaesthetic during that long flight south from Dien Bien Phu, called: '*Wotan song – one, two, three*!'

As one, three hundred hoarse young voices burst into the old marching song in German, which echoed a brutal pride in what they were and had once been in another war. On the dais the new boys, who had fought them in that war, blanched and looked shocked. But the singing men cared nothing for them or their feelings; they roared out those words, as if to challenge the whole world:

> *Blow the bugle, beat the drum!*
> *Clear the street, here comes Wo-tan!*
> *Steel is our weapon*
> *To hew through bone.*
> *Blood our purpose,*
> *Wotan hold close.*
> *For Death is our Destiny . . .*

And then the Headhunters were gone; they had vanished from the shocked gaze of the new boys, leaving the silence to echo behind them . . .

All Futura Books are available at your bookshop or
newsagent, or can be ordered from the following
address:
Futura Books, Cash Sales Department,
P.O. Box 11, Falmouth, Cornwall.

Please send cheque or postal order (no currency), and
allow 40p for postage and packing for the first book
plus 18p for the second book and 13p for each additional
book ordered up to a maximum charge of £1.49 in U.K.

Customers in Eire and B.F.P.O. please allow 40p for
the first book, 18p for the second book plus 13p per
copy for the next 7 books, thereafter 7p per book.

Overseas customers please allow 60p for postage and
packing for the first book and 18p per copy for each
additional book.

15 48 / 5 1